LOVE
THAT TRANSCENDS TIME

BY

K S MICHAELS

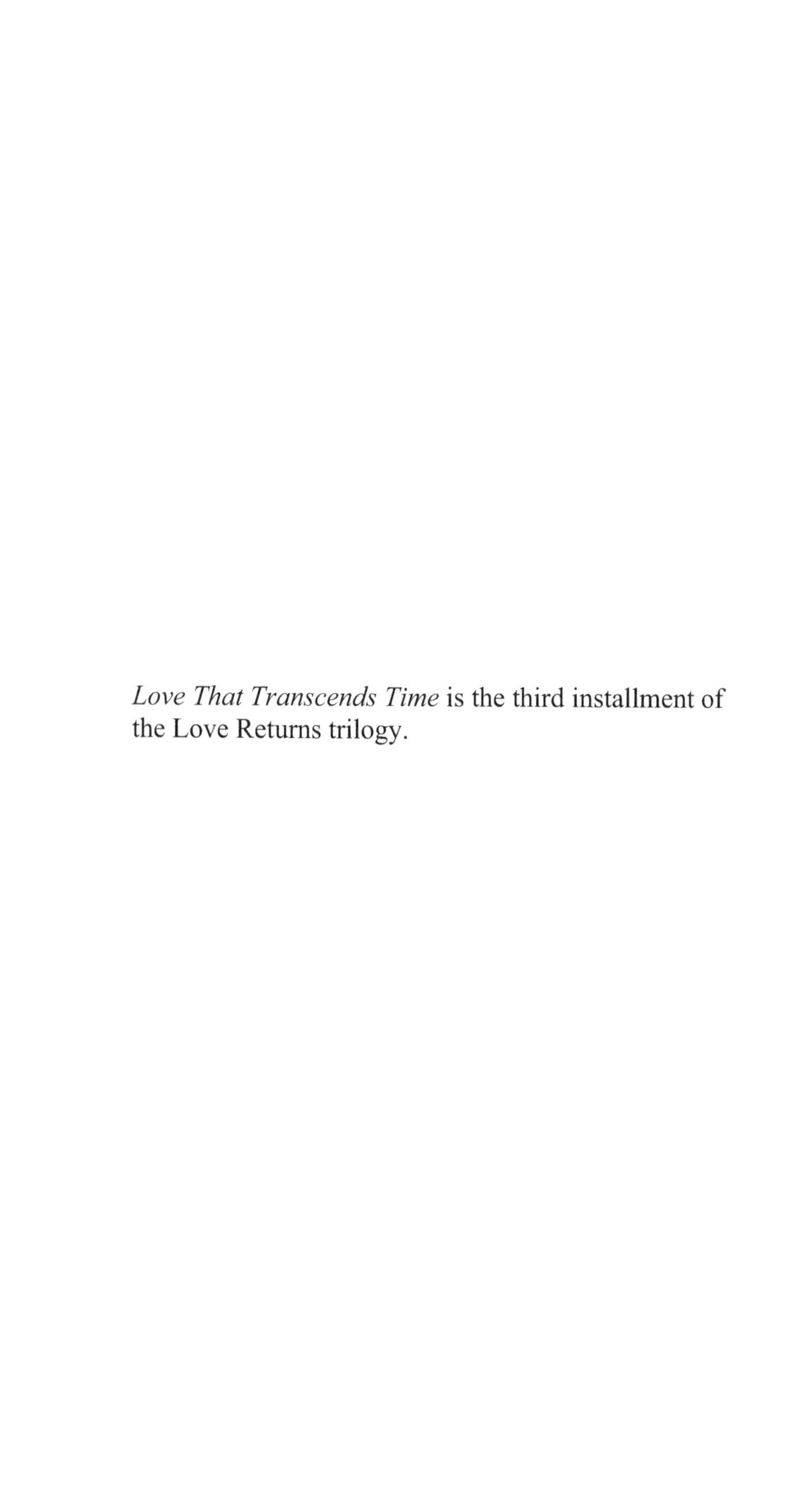

Love That Transcends Time is the third installment of the Love Returns trilogy.

TABLE OF CONTENTS

Introduction

The Soul by Samantha Shane
Age 15

"The soul.   We generally refer to our inner self as the soul.   The dictionary describes our soul as a **nonphysical aspect of a person:** the complex of human attributes that manifests as consciousness, thought, feeling, and will, regarded as distinct from the physical body.
Distinct from the physical body…even the dictionary claims a separation between body and soul.
Scientists have already documented a body that had just died was suddenly twenty-one grams lighter the moment death occurred.   This proven fact has been studied and witnessed more than once.   This study, first, dates back to 1907.   The calculations were similar every time, and all instrument calibrations were conducted before and after the experiment.
So I ask you, where did the soul go?   Do you doubt the scientific tests to be valid?   Do you believe the soul simply floated away into oblivion never to been heard from again?   Do souls float into space to become something we know nothing about?   Do souls become our guardian angels?   Do they simply roam the Earth aimlessly?   If they remain Earthbound, are they aware of us?   Do you believe in reincarnation?   Do you believe in ghosts, spirits, poltergeists or haunting?   If so, do you suppose the soul returns to a new body some time in the future?
How many souls do think there might be?
According to some, the guff is a limited number of souls waiting to experience life in the physical form. And once the guff is depleted mankind will have reached his time; time for the apocalypse.
Some claim death is final, no returns, no passing GO and collecting $200.00, no experiences to recall and no existence whatsoever, here or anywhere, forever.

The concept of finality to non-existence from corporeal form, to me, is less acceptable than any pain I have yet to experience.
Many people who have had Near Death Experiences (NDE) claim that they saw a bright light while feeling pulled to a destination.   They also claimed that the pain and suffering that plagued them in life had not only vanished, but their state of mind and psyche had completely transformed to a halcyon calm that they vaguely remember feeling, but not from a time when they were alive.   Others who have had NDE say they had felt not only the absence of pain, but a sense of nirvana so strong that they actually regretted coming back when revived.   Others who were able to recollect their NDE after being revived wanted nothing more than to return to what they considered to be home, a higher, sacred place.
Could it have been heaven?   Does that mean there is a Hell?   Does that confirm there is a God?
My NDE was somewhat different from these said accounts.   My death was not a painful one.   I suffer from a heart disorder.   My disorder is congenital. When my first death experience came I was fully aware of my predicament.   (I omit the word *near* because I was clinically dead just like so many others.)   I don't believe there is anything *nearer* to death than death itself.   Like many others, I had been revived.   But had I not been revived, death was certain.

        My death was slow to occur.   I was passively falling into a sleep stasis as my heart simply stopped functioning properly.   There was some discomfort by nothing compared to so many other's NDE.   My fondest memory of death was the nirvana.   I felt it immediately.   I concur with others who felt disappointed to be revived.   Though I am fond of life and would choose to be alive, I can see how many would choose otherwise.   If this nirvana were to come in a pill form, I doubt anyone would be able to keep from becoming a junkie once tried and experienced.   Aside from the wondrous calm of elated spirits and the dearth of discomfort, I recall very little else.   Perhaps time is relevant when dead. Maybe I wasn't dead long enough to know what more was to come.   It took the paramedics around three minutes to revive me from the grasp of my demise.

I have spoken with many who claim to have experienced the nirvana.   Each one of them claim that they have never again felt anything close.

In my case, I have felt it on many occasions while still alive.   I don't know what brought it on.   I don't know if or when it will ever happen again. But I do know, the feeling is like nothing I could possibly explain in words.   I had once fallen to my knees with pleasure permeating my body and mind. It was like suddenly being overdosed by an explosion of endorphins.   Both physical and mental sensors were misfiring all at once.   Not that any of this would necessarily be a bad experience, however, imagine (as best you could) having an orgasm, falling in love and winning the lottery all at once.   The sensory overload of such an event would not be my concern…to the contrary; it would be the recovery from such an experience that worries me.   I still remember how it made me feel, each time, exactly the same and just as powerful.   How does one recover from this without wanting to go back?   Do I invite death?   Absolutely not.   Because of my heart condition, I know I have a purpose and a foreseeable journey that has yet to be fulfilled.   I believe I have a mission to complete by helping others who suffer from a terminal illness as I do.   But I can say without reservation, I do not fear death.   However, I

do not live fearlessly absent of caution.   I simply
live each day to the fullest, but not as though it were
my last, of course…I do have a retirement plan.
For those who face the terminal inevitability, I say,
"fear not.   Know there is love beyond the stars."

CHAPTER 1
Samantha is realized

After Rosemary's passing, Miranda would
frequently attempt to ease Samantha's (Sam) mind by
spending a lot of time with her alone, taking her out
to various places like the park or the mall.   At age
six, Sam was a very influential child.   Three months
since the funeral, Sam had yet to show her emotions.
She hadn't yet cried or even spoken of Rosemary
except to say how much she missed her.   It was as if
she had already accepted the reality of the situation.
Or my suspicions of the other side are more
prominent to the young at heart than first thought to
be.   Sam missed the hugs and the physical aspect of
Rosemary's company, but I strongly believed the
communications between the two must have,
somehow, continued via a spiritual symbiosis.
None of which would surprise me or her mom.
Granted, Miranda and I are not your average couple.
And no doubt, our little girl shares many of our

unique qualities.   I could easily understand how she would be able to overcome sorrow and acclimate accordingly.   She had an amazing intellect accompanied by her own powerful mystical abilities.   However, one day in the park would prove my young daughter, Samantha a power to be reckoned with.   Oddly, I was not too surprised to hear Miranda tell me of the event.   And yet, I temporarily shuttered while gestating the proper course of action to take.   As a child prodigy, I dare not inhibit Sam's gifted abilities.   I am a firm believer in the development of the mind and all that is considered.   My young daughter loves to read.   So I give her books enough to her heart's content.   Whatever the cost or the trouble to procure the titles she finds interest in, I make it happen.   I want no limits to bind my child's growth.   However, a six year old with supernatural powers enough to cause injury to others, demands that I must take precautions when raising my child.   What Sam did at the park was unacceptable.   The day she was born, my gut instincts told me she would be a handful.   On the other hand, I couldn't be more proud and fully interested in just how much power this amazing child had and would be able to enhance.

It was the perfect day for an outing at the park.   The sky was absent of the usual encroaching smog from the San Fernando Valley.   The joggers were trekking along the path clad in shorts and tank-tops with ear-plugs in and wrist and headbands for fashion.
The smell of the freshly cut grass would remind Miranda of her days as a child when one of her weekly chores would be to mow the lawn and dump the house-trash.   Regardless of the fact she had no older brothers, her father insisted she be raised as an equal.   He saw no reason why he should expect her

to be treated differently.   He despised a woman who couldn't change a tire or fill the radiator when needed.

I believed he was a wise man.   I could appreciate the fine qualities he instilled in my lovely wife. Though I often referred to her as my little grease monkey, I could not have been more proud of her.   I knew I didn't need to worry about her abilities or security when we were apart.   As a capable family manager, a loving mother and a best friend and wife to me I knew, with her help, we would be able to figure out a suitable plan for Samantha.

When the two girls got to the park it had already been filled with mommies and kids.   Some were the regulars, others were first time curiosities. Miranda took a seat on a bench facing the swings. Sam would almost always gravitate to the swings. I once witnessed Sam fade into her meditative state while swinging in the back yard of our home.   I could see and feel her move from one level of consciousness to another with little effort as she would swing through the air, eyes filled with pure joy.   Her aura would glow to a blinding incandescence.   Like a brand new battery, Sam would come away from her swing recharged with ideas and plans that would amaze me and her mom to no end.   I would catch myself talking with her as though she were a mature adult mapping out her itinerary for her retirement years.   She was like no other, much less, any known six year old.   It took me years to accomplish what Miranda had taught her in weeks.   To achieve and embark on a meditative state to which the levels are of the highest of consciousness is an astounding undertaking.   Sam excels where most fail and others can hardly maintain the pace in which she finds comfortable and natural.

Kids were running about in random directions.   Some on the monkey bars, some having fun on the slide.   All the swings were in use as Sam stood patiently in a line of five others waiting her turn.   Oddly, there were only six swings in the park for a neighborhood of, what seemed to be, millions of children.   As Sam finally made it to the front of the line her wait became unusually long.   The last six children on the swings were less likely to relinquish their seats than the others.

A young boy who had been on the swings the longest took notice of Sam waiting patiently for her turn.

As Miranda had described the event to me later that day, the boy seemed to take pleasure in taunting Sam who gave no reason to cause his little tease.   The boy seemed to be around eight or nine. He had a turned up nose and wore his straight hair short with bangs.   Sam gave little notice when the boy would stick his tongue out at her.   When he realized he could not get a rise out of her he decided to badger her with name calling.   Seemingly, a typical child of his age.   Perhaps he liked her, thought she was cute.

Miranda was especially proud of her daughter when Sam continued to give no response.

When the other children on the swings noticed what was happening, they too decided to join in with the taunting.   Why kids act the way they do is beyond me.   Many of these same children had played in the park many times before with Sam.

Miranda could see the anger beginning to build and fester within Sam's little face and eyes. She took the opportunity to watch and see what Sam would do.   Usually, Sam would be quite diplomatic in such situations, but of course, these were little kids and not the adults she was accustomed to reasoning with.   As all the children joined in with a terribly nasty chant, "Ugly pig can't go on the swings…ugly pig can't go on the swings…" Sam continued to show little concern.   To only those who knew her well, she appeared to slip into one of her distant stares, a trance of a pleasant calm.

The little boy who started the little taunting took extra gratification in getting his little friends to join in.   But what he saw next had him pinned with curiosity.   He was on the third swing from where Sam was standing.

Slowly and calm, while staring ahead and seeming as though she were in a trance or even sleep walking with her eyes wide open, Sam walked across the front of the first two swings until she reached the third.   Just inches from being kicked by the children, she reached the third swing and stopped.   She turned her body in a slow robotic motion to face the little boy.

He was the first to slow the chant to a halt as his voice cracked the last note.   And as the other children followed suit, Sam stared directly into the little boy's eyes.   She spoke low and very distinct, "I want to swing on the swing."

"That's too darn bad, ugly pig-girl." said the little boy, sticking his tongue out.

"I want to swing on this swing."   Sam said, slow to lift her arm, pointing a finger directly at the little boy.

First, the boy began to laugh, then he bravely incited another childish chant, "You can't have it…you can't have it…"

This time, the other children would not join. Whatever they might have been thinking, it was obvious to Miranda that the other children could see that Sam meant business.

"I want your swing and I want it now."   Sam

demanded, keeping her steady stare.   Her face was like stone, and her arm never lowered.

With a shivering chill that rushed over Miranda's entire body in a flash, she knew just what was to occur next.   There was nothing she could do without drawing too much attention to herself and her daughter.   Nothing she might have done would have changed the end-result anyhow.   The hair on her arms stood on end with an electrical surge.

The two kids swinging on both sides of the little boy dragged their feet through the sand in an attempt to stop as soon as they possibly could.   One jumped off when he could not make his swing stop fast enough.   The other managed to halt the swing but could not keep herself from crying as she ran from the swing pit straight to her mom.   Aside from Miranda, not one parent seemed to know what was going on.   Occupied by novels or the deep thought of common stresses, who knows what kept others from seeing what was so obvious to Miranda.

"You are a very mean boy."   Sam said, nodding her head ever so slowly.

In an instant the boy stopped his last chant. His attention was drawn into her steadfast eyes that didn't blink or look away.

"And you are a very ugly girl." said the boy with a slight stutter to his voice.   The momentum of his swing suddenly began to slow as he stopped pumping his legs and paid strict attention to Sam's impaling eyes.

"You shouldn't say mean things to people." Sam lowered her arm.   "Someday, somebody or something might beat you up."

The boy made every effort to hide his fear and maintain his rant.   But he could not find his voice. He could not get the words out no matter how hard he tried.   He was barely able to stick his tongue out at her as his face flushed with a blanket of paralyzing fear.   His cheeks turned red as though it were a cold winter day.   His eyes filled with emotions he could not hide.   Absent of all his banter, the little boy could not take his eyes from hers.

Sam never moved a muscle.   No one was within earshot to know what was happening.   The remaining children on the swings had already slipped away undetected.

The laughter and voices of the people in the park seemed to fade silent in the distance.   The little boy's swing slowly came to a halt.   His feet dragged through the sand one last time.

Sam stepped forward and whispered into the little boy's ear, "Now you know what it's like to get beat up by an 'ugly' six-year-old girl."

A trickle of blood streamed from the boy's left nostril past his lips and chin.

"Now get off my swing." said Sam, with a stern growling voice.

As if to be suddenly released from a shackling spell, the little boy was able to find his feet and run off as fast as his legs could carry him without a word or a whimper.

As Miranda went into detail describing all that she witnessed and felt, we both knew it was time to a have a serious talk with our daughter.   What she did to the little boy was far more than what was seen on the surface.   She managed to instill fear in the mind of that little boy by way of a mystic's process most mediums would have little success at summoning.   Though Miranda was at least a hundred feet from her daughter, she felt every nuance that was taking place across the green.

What Miranda told me next created a chill that ran up the nape of my neck as well.   She described exactly how Sam had scared that little boy into believing she was his worst nightmare. Everything that little boy had envisioned, Miranda was able to view as well, and describe to me.   Sam's entire façade had magically disfigured into what resembled a wicked old dried apple face.   But the retaliation did not stop there.   That unfortunate little boy might have been psychologically scarred for life for all I know.   He didn't just runaway with two smacked cheeks, a bloody nose and a wet pair of shorts.   He truly believed he saw a little girl morph into a very formidable witch.   And within less than thirty seconds she had him believing she had cast a spell over him, taking him from the security of his surroundings and lunging him into her world of frightening ugliness.

I could only imagine the story that child might have tried to tell his parents.   Though I was a bit relieved knowing his folks would not believe him, I couldn't help but feel a bit sorry for him as well.   Though he was, no doubt a brat, what right did Samantha have traumatizing him in such a frightful manner?   Our work was cut out for us.   That was for sure.   I remember when I was a kid reading the old Spiderman magazines.   Remembering what the Uncle said to his nephew, trying to guide him and explain the responsibility involved with having great powers.   Though my little girl was only six, and obviously old enough and gifted enough to summon such powers, I should have been able to convey the same importance to her as the Uncle did.   It would seem a silly analogy but it was the only training I had in this field.   I wasn't raised with gifted parents. And I certainly didn't have anyone to talk to concerning my abilities or questions.   *I wondered if Stan Lee had any super natural gifts of his own.*

CHAPTER 2
Mike is realized

"It's not like the boy didn't deserve to get his butt kicked--" I sometimes…okay, always, take a defensive point of view on behalf of my daughter.

"Babe," She cast a look to me that begged to be reckoned with.   "She didn't even get on the swing after the boy ran away."   Miranda said, sounding annoyed with my one-sided view point. "Our daughter was very satisfied with herself.   I told her what she did was wrong, and that we would need to have a talk about it tonight.   We need to address this immediately."

"I know, you're right.   We definitely need to nip this in the 'butt' before it gets out of hand."

"Bud." Miranda corrected.

"What?"

"You said, 'butt'.   The correct phrase is supposed to be 'bud'."

"Now why would anyone want to nip at a bud.   I much prefer to nip at butts.   What a stupid expression."

"Wow," Miranda sarcastically remarked. "And to think--not only did you actually take the time to think that one through, but that was the best you could do?   I'm trying to be serious here."

"Seriously, I could bite something else, if you prefer." Sometimes, I think I just like to tease her for no reason at all.

"Perhaps later, Romeo.   Right now we have business with our daughter."

"Buzz-kill." I tittered, while pinching at her bottom. "Nip, nip, nip."

She was right though, Samantha displayed powers we never realized she had. No doubt, she was a force to be reckoned with. I had always sensed she would be the one to watch for. From the very first day I held her in my arms, I could see her eyes reading me through and through. I strongly believed she and I were carrying on conversations with just our eyes. And now, like teachers for the super natural, we had to redirect her energies, find her center and evoke a positive and more passive lifestyle. I hated to impede such a gift. But I would never forgive myself if any harm were to come to her. And I don't mean harm by way of other kids. My main concern was for those who might be watching. Perhaps one could call me a bit paranoid. But it's only because I have good reason. I have seen what can happen to others and their gifts. If they are not made to look like fools or opportunists for all the public to see, they are made out to be shysters and thieves out for monetary gain at the expense of the believing public. And if that isn't the worst, I would be willing to bet on what the government would do to my little girl if they could get their own greedy hands on her. I wasn't about to let my Samantha be poked and prodded. In the name of "National Security", we would never be allowed to see our little girl again. Living on the run would be last thing I wanted for my family. Somehow, I knew we would need to convey the importance of our family secret to her. And though she was only six at the time, I figured if she was able to use her powers for the wrong reasons, we should be able to show her the path to the right one's. Besides, I had learned from many different entities that the best way to hide something important was to keep it in plain view.

Hiding something in plain view was nothing new through the course of history.   Many people never knew or even would have guessed that Jules Verne was a medium, a very powerful medium, in fact. And what did he do to hide his talent?   He wrote books about it.   Talk about hiding his gift in plain view.   H. G. Wells was born in 1866 England. Though they didn't burn the heretics at the stake in his era, they didn't mind hanging them and hang them they did.   He had to be especially careful to hide his craft as well.   Though he did it with a reversed psychology that amazes historians to this day.   Instead of taking the chance and risking his life like Nostradamus did with overt predictions of kings and queens, Wells wrote book after book exploring his craft of predictions in stories of fiction. Even today, so many people seem to think he was an amazing scholar of science and invention.   Okay, so he was quite a scholar of science and invention. And, no doubt, his penchant was keeping up with the times of progress.   But, no scientists of the early nineteen hundreds could have possibly known of Wells' predictions to be the unfolding truth behind such machines as wireless phones and genetically engineered animals.   Wells predicted a science that didn't exist until years after his death.   Lucky guesses, or perhaps really good ideas?   Who knows what they thought back then?   Who would have thought up the laser (a bright silent light of intense heat) had it not been for this man?   He used his gift to further his gains.   And, he obviously enjoyed his craft, power to him.   Or as Rose would say "Bully for you."

And what about Jules Verne?   Talk about the Master of Science.   I believe Verne to be a genius.   His novels revealed his predictions of such things as the submarine, solar cells and variety of weapons used today, but too far-fetched for yesterday.   Traveling to the moon wasn't too extreme for Jules Verne either.

There are a number of ways to hide in plain sight. And I'm not talking camouflage.

    "But he deserved it!" Sam demanded adamantly.

    I didn't dare butt in, though my expression may have agreed with my little girl.

    "Yes, but there are right ways of doing things and wrong ways."   Miranda began her speech on being the good little girl and how not to act out our anger.   As she continued on with the proper way to act like a lady, I had to, finally, step in.   I could see this line of reasoning would have taken all night at this rate.

    "Honey, you are a very gifted child.   You have heard me say this time and time again.   And I am very proud of you.   However, there a some not so good people who might want to steal your gift from you, which also means taking you away from us--"

    "Babe?"   Miranda said, browbeating me. "Aren't we being a bit harsh, HONEY?"

    "Well, I see no reason to beat around the bush.   She gets it…"

    "Yeah, Mom.   I think I get it.   I shouldn't be doing any magic in front of people like that little snotty boy because some bad guys might want to steal me away, take me to Los Vegas and force me to do card counting."

    "Card counting?"   looking quite astounded, Miranda glared directly at me.

    "Hey don't look at me, she's your daughter

too. I don't know where she gets this stuff."   I winked at my little girl sealing our secret.

With a sidelong glance she continued, "Yeah, okay, Elvis who has been banned from Vegas, and we won't say why."

I just shook my head acting quite confused at Sam who seemed to be enjoying our playful bicker.

"On the serious side," Miranda intoned.   "It just isn't safe to allow anyone to know what you are capable of.   Besides, you could have really hurt that little boy.   We are not bad people who hurt one another.   We help people. That's why we have been given such a wonderful gift."

"Yeah, well somebody forgot to tell that to Mike Simon."   Mike Simon was a guy who was found to have super natural healing powers projected through the magnetism in his hands.   He once used his prowess to heal a young five year-old child from Leukemia who was said to be on her deathbed with less than hours to live.   It took him less than an hour to heal her with just his touch.
However, Mike also learned that he could use his magnetism to control the roll of the slot machines at the Stardust.   Much like Uri Geller, the self proclaimed psychic and illusionist who could bend spoons with his mind, Mike could somehow read the roll of the machines simply by placing his hand on the side of the machine to influence its speed and momentum.   Needles to say, neither of us are allowed back at the Stardust.   And believe me, you don't want to meet Bruno Tuscola down in the basement of that hotel without reservations, if you know what I mean.

"Honey?"   *Miranda puts up with so much from me.   I don't know how she does it.   I really don't.*

"Sorry."

Sam chuckled, though I doubt she knew who Mike Simon was.   She has always been my best audience.

"Just make sure it doesn't happen again, Sam.   It is important that you understand just how serious we really are about this subject.   Terrible things can happen if you continue to abuse your gift in this manner, again."

"Okay, Mommy I promise."   her pensive little frown was, no doubt, a façade for what she saw coming from her mom next.

"Do you remember the time when you had to write me a story because we found that your pre-school teacher was upset with you when you tried to help her with her personal problem?"

"I was only trying to help her."   Sam still felt somewhat cheated for that one.   Her teacher really did have a drinking problem.   The fact that Sam helped her by allowing her to know that her teacher's dad did not blame her for his death may have been a bit frightening coming from a four year-old.   But at least the end result was favorable.   And Miss Gomez did, in fact, stop drinking after that awkward event.

"I know honey, you intended to do a good thing, but we still insist you don't allow people to see what we can do.   You know there are better ways to handle such things.   So, to show me that you truly understand, I would like you to write me story depicting what you did to that little boy, and why it was wrong to do so.   Will you do that for me?"   So maternal is my sweet wife.   I never would have thought of that as a punishment.

"Yes, Mommy.   I will write you a story. How long does it have to be?"   Sam crossed her arms showing her unfavorable mood swing.

"Just a page, like before."

One would think this task might be a bit too harsh for a child of only six, however, we both knew that Sam loved to write.   And the things she had written about would, many times, blow me away. Sam will one day be one of the greatest philosophers on this planet.   Mark my words, I have told all my friends, she's the next Khalil Gibran watch and see.

The following morning I woke to find Samantha's story on the kitchen counter just as requested.   I couldn't wait to heat up some hot chocolate, sit outside on the deck by the oak tree and read my child's perspective of what transpired the day before.   Without having yet read the story I had to chuckle to myself as I remembered her last story of resentment and sarcasm.   Needless to say, Mommy had her rewrite that story until Sam saw things our way.
She titled the story; A Bit Of a Pig.   Already, she had me grinning from ear to ear.   I could already feel the sarcasm dripping from the paper.
The story read;
He called me a pig.   Imagine that.   Well then, if you wish, you may picture me to be a bit of a pig. So be it.   It hasn't fractured me.   In fact, a pig is quite a vivid imagination.   He really had a way with his expression or perception.   And if he still had this picture fresh in his mind, please allow me to assist you in some minor details.
I possess four-hundred sixty-nine pounds of piggy meat on my bones.   I don't walk very fast.   Never do I run.   Eating has become one of my favorite past times, with sleeping as my other.   I just adore the genuine sincerity and innocents of little piglets.
Perhaps I should be in search of a mate before my slaughter.   I would like my mate dressed in a red ribbon and a smile.   Today, I like red.   I think red

may be my sexual stimulant as well as nakedness.   I
would like to make noises when I mate, loud grunting
noises with lots of heavy gasps.
My body is covered with sparse, course, kinky short
blond hairs, exposing most of my pinkish skin, like a
precious, new-born baby rat.
An unusual thing happened to me today; I grew
wings…large wings.   And my pudgy, stout little
hooves grew strong, sharpened talons.   The hair
turned to feathers.   I also became aware of my
feculent surroundings, at which time my body
became firm and muscularly.   All the lard of my
shell had unfurled into a hard fortress of scales
beneath my regal display of soft feathers.   As I
became able to stand erect upon my hind legs, my tail
grew long, and narrow like a whip.   At the end of
my tail grew sharp pernicious spikes filled with
deadly injections.   My hubris exploded into an
impromptu dance of arrogance and physical power.
My every movement was lionized with physical
prowess and grace.   I could feel the earth tremble
beneath my steps.   The strength in my legs enabled
me to jump to heights that before were only
imaginable.   I was suddenly able to see the rooftops
of all the surrounding buildings and structures.   I
saw places I never knew existed.   As my dutiful legs
met with the ground once more, I pushed off with
greater force than before.   The ground rumbled like
the onset of an earthquake.   The incessant growth of
my power coaxed me on with an insatiable hunger for
more.   The energy of my powers projected me
higher than before.   The speed of assent continued
to accelerate, past the rooftops, past the neighborhood
sights.   Fear never entered my mind.   High in the
sky, just beneath the clouds, the force of my thrust
finally reached the summit, and without a second
thought, my innate nature of anew rose to a skillful

display of my stalwart wings as they unfolded from behind my back and spread across the sky.   Before the downfall ever could take effect, the updraft of my flight took to the air on the breeze that carried me effortlessly.   My massive shadow engulfed buildings and streets alike.   The sensation was magnificent as it was euphoric.   My random course would glide across the sky, passing over entire cities in mere seconds.   With the wind beneath my wings created an unheard of speed that would accrue like a jet after takeoff.   The metamorphosis of my body continued while I was I flight.   The blunt of my nose stretched further from my face.   The nostrils became small and had formed to the sides of what seemed to become a sallow, hook-shaped bill with a razor sharp bite.   I could feel the stretching tension at my face as the brow of my nose augmented to final form.   My cheek bones molded like clay before my eyes.   If the beast within me were to be given a name, I might have called myself a Griffin.
Inherent experimentation urged me to excel in speed. I was fully aerodynamic. With deft powerful strokes, I pulled my wings in beneath my torso and back out with a thrust of expansion that had me soaring across the sky like magic.   My body cut through the wind with a razor sharp motion.   Every stroke of my massive wings brought greater speed and gratification.   I felt the warming friction of the air licking at my body as I continued to soar to adventure.   As I looked down upon the tiny town below, I could see the many people far in the distance.   I descended for a closer look.   My shadow spanned across an entire highway.   As I would pass over, my image would darken the streets causing and interest from those who took notice.   I could read their thoughts as plain as reading a map. Their eyes filled with fear upon first glance.   Some

just stood palsied.   And I fed on their consternation.
I enjoyed the prerogative new.   And then, quite
suddenly, it occurred to me.   As I flew over a small
house just outside of my town, I saw a familiar face.
A face that brought anger and discomfort to me.   It
was he, the opinionated one, the one who called me a
pig.   Before I could call upon my senses, instinct
possessed me in an instant.   My fury took control
over me.   In a flash, I had descended upon him.   It
was all so natural and instinctual a response.   With
wings splayed fully, perhaps twenty feet across, my
talons reached from beneath me into a forward
motion.   Clasping both his shoulders in my vice-
gripped talons, I swept him up off his feet.   As
graceful as a well guided kite on the beach, I
succeeded in snaring my prey and escalated to a
height hundreds of feet over his home in just two
strokes of my almighty wings.   I could feel the
pierce of my talons impaling through his shirt into his
flesh.   The milksop of a man whimpered and cried
out in pain.   Stirring thoughts filled my mind.   Oh,
what great pain I could inflict.   He has not yet begun
to imagine what I could do.   I could have simply
dropped him just to watch him splat on the sidewalk.
What satisfaction I gained from hearing his
whimpering grovel.   What thrills I nurtured as I
ascended higher into the surrounding of nothingness.

        "Oh God, don't let me die." he said, with
tears making their path down his cheeks onto his
bloody shirt.   The words from his lips hit me
unrepentantly hard.   I felt as though some swaging
force was reigning back my rage.   My onslaught fell
uncertain.   His cries that once coaxed me, now were
crippling me like kryptonite to Superman.   Bitter
hatred was dissipating at an accelerated rate.   I
could not account for this.   The cogency of such a
plead was unmatched by any I could have believed.

My heinous adventure weakened with every fleeting
moment.
His plea penetrated then infiltrated my every defense.
I soon learned that my fortress of body armor was
obviously not the answer for my virtues.
He hadn't yet noticed that we had descended back to
the ground until he felt his feet scuffling along the
ground just prior to my releasing him in front of his
home.
It was made quite clear to me then.   And I thanked
God as well.

        At the bottom of the page Samantha had left
her mom a humorous note.

        Hey Mom, why do Firemen use Dalmatians?
Give up?   Because in the event of a fire, they are
easier to spot.   Tee hee.

        "Oh, boy", was all I could say.   I read it
twice.   And to think she had just turned six.
Perhaps a bit too much use of the thesaurus, but very
interesting just the same.
        Okay, Mom had a lot to do with her amazing
brilliance.   She was taught to read when most kids
were still learning to poop in the toilet.   When most
kids were watching Sesame Street on the television,
Samantha was mesmerized by the writings of Edgar
Allen Poe, as her Mom would read to her each day.
I suppose her being in the best private school in the
county had a lot to do with my little prodigy, as well.
Do I sound like a proud daddy?   Heh, you bet.
        Oh, by the way, I was just recently informed
by my, soon to be, brother-in-law, Bradley that Edgar
Allen Poe was a self- published writer due to the fact,
not one of the publishing agencies of his time found
his work worthy of printing.   And yes, there is a

relevance to this trivia fact.   Thanks to Bradley, I was also able to put a few mysteries of my own to rest.

Night after night, I would awake to Miranda's soothing voice attempting to calm my night chilled hysterics.   The dreams grew to a near overwhelming preoccupation of attempting to decipher some redeeming interpretation.   Generally, I had little trouble predicting immediate trouble while going about my day.   But by night, when asleep, my mind would seemingly fall prey to a labyrinth of confusion and misguided signals with little insight as to what the message was attempting to tell me.   I nearly dreaded sleeping many nights lest I would not be able to foresee and understand the danger that or I my family might be facing.   I hated feeling as though my hands were tied.   I was at wit's end and exhausted suffering from sleep deprivation when one day Bradley's insight had offered me, what I thought was, absolute resolve.   So unexpected, the information he shared was literally like a message in a bottle set adrift mid-sea hoping I would be saved. My dreams would, each time, culminate with that very scene, me adrift at sea.   From one moment to another the scenario would skip from one extreme to another.   I would find my sails unfurled by an eternal dead calm.   The pounding heat of the sun had me baked and potentially left for dead.   There was positively no land in sight, and no refuge from the scorching heat.   I had cast a bottle with a note inside, my last *Will and Testament* from Mike Shane. Then, suddenly, I would find myself caught in a rogue wave that would hurl me into a maelstrom that seemingly came from the belly of the sea with Peter Walbrook as Poseidon rising from the tumultuous sea, blowing me into a swirl, funneling me to the bottom of the ocean floor and never to be seen again.

Knowing that Peter was safely tucked away in jail I
couldn't possibly believe that he had anything to do
with my ill-fated warnings.   Or so I thought.   How
naive could I have been?
Bradley's uncanny memory storage of facts came to
my rescue when he so simply and frankly put two
and two together.   Like a mathematician, he put
together the relevance.   And *together*, we sought the
plot that plagued my dreams like warning signs on
the highway.   In my dream, I put my last will and
testament adrift in a bottle that served me as my last
drink before my demise.   Edgar Allen Poe lived a
life of destitution and unfortunate circumstances.
Bradley was an avid reader of, laterally or *(literary)*
thousands of prophetic writers of historic influence.
We discovered that Poe's writings and his life story
was especially cogent in theory to the subject at hand.
And I am not one to be taken by surprise or easily
amazed by uncanny coincidences.   But when I
learned that Edgar Allen Poe, who lived and died
decades before my grandparents were born, had
written an award winning literary story about my life,
it made the hair on my arms stand on end and chills
run through the back of my neck.   Yes, Mike Shane,
me.   The title of Poe's story published in 1833 was
called, "MS Found in a Bottle."   The story's horror
comes from its scientific imaginings and its
description of a physical world beyond the limits of
human exploration.

   As Bradley had further explained to me, Poe was a
most unfortunate man battered by both his bad
choices and the jealousies of others who wished to
possess such a talent as his.   Writers and scholars
such as H. G. Well and Jules Verne were deeply
influenced by the amazing works of Poe.   Verne
would actually write a sequel to one of Poe's books.
Sadly, soon after Poe's death one terrible foe named

Rufus Wilmot Griswold had written and published a terrible biography on Poe depicting him as a drug addict and horrible man of plagiarism and poor insight.   Fortunately, Poe's closest friends redeemed his reputation in the end.

All evidence provided by Bradley's phenomenal mind helped me to understand more than I realized could possibly have been happening to me.   I knew that Peter had it in for me.   That was no surprise to me.   He proved that to me when I first discovered that he was the one that was responsible for stealing a manuscript of mine.   However, with him in jail for a good, long time I hardly saw the threat that would soon be revealed to us all.   Peter's bitter jealousy went far deeper than I first imagined.   I never should have doubted Crystal's many hints and warnings.

It took some work, but via Miranda's amazing abilities and Bradley's fortitude we were able to ferret out just what Peter had done to undermine my own literary work.   I have to admit, to have come up with such a devious plan took true genius.   If this man were to redirect his talent to the positive force instead of the *dark side*, he could have easily made himself a legit fortune.   But as Crystal had, many times, warned, he is not the type to adhere to legitimacy.   In his own distorted way of thinking, he believed that I had taken Crystal's love from him and therefore I was to be punished just like anyone else who might get caught in his path of what he calls success via devious cheatings.   As if to say, honesty was too simple, and cheating was honorable and highly regarded as clever mastery, resigned only for those who appreciate stepping on others to get their way.   What a shame and waste of such talent was I could think of for this unfortunate man.

As Peter found resolve in directing his attention

toward destroying my reputation as a writer, similar to what happened to Poe, Peter had purchased a copy of my first novel after it had been first published. He cleverly hired a print shop to make one-thousand copies of the book to look almost identical to mine. Identical to those who wouldn't know any better. Or think to look for any differences.   I, certainly, never noticed.   However, Peter did the unthinkable. What kind of a mind would come up with such a devious plot was beyond my imagination.   With little regard for his out-of-pocket expenses or payment for his troubles, Peter commissioned a writer to literally rewrite the entire book riddled with misspelled words, misuse of words, and a horrific distortion to the story plot.   Such a serious injustice to a work that represented the very epitome of love and peace. *Love Returns Through The Portal of Time* was my baby, my first attempt at telling the world that love is abound if we'd only open our eyes and heart to the many possibilities.   Such a personal attack on something so defenseless, I thought his plot to be nothing less than unconscionable.

"You need to understand that, underneath it all, Peter is nothing more than a coward and thief." The words that Crystal had warned would ring in my ears over again.

When Peter's rewrite of my book was done, the new copies looked to be written by an illiterate drunk. But, what he did next was deplorable and a most personal attack on all of us involved.   He sent all the books, but fifty, to a partnership business that dealt solely in shipping products.   Peter then instructed the company to sell all the books back to every bookstore that supplied my original story sparing no cost for free shipping to the buyer.   But to add insult to injury, he priced all the books at one penny. According to Crystal, Peter was broke and destitute at the time he was incarcerated, so where he got the money to pull off such costly attack was a curiosity to all of us.   On the other hand, a man behind bars can be quite dangerous via his connections, but a dangerous man with money, caught behind bars can be far more connected than I cared to think about. Bradley calculated Peter's cost for such a devious plan might have cost him as much as six grand to pull off.

We later found that the last fifty copies had been distributed to all the local Libraries free of cost to the public.   Somehow, I figured, Peter wasn't as bad off, financially, as Crystal might have thought.   He was pretty good at hiding things like contracts and guns.   Who's to say he didn't keep an offshore account ready at standby?   It seemed like his rainy day to me.

To this day, I still see some of his books, under my name, being circulated in bookstores all over.   And there isn't a thing I can do about it.   I could see by many of the reviews of irate readers, Peter's plan seems to have worked.   Though they might have only paid a penny, some chose to resell the book at the publisher's original price.   Heck, I would be upset too if I "shelled out" good money for a book of gibberish.

However, I can offer a bit of remedy to those who still possess a copy of Peter's deception…perhaps one day it will become a collector's item worth more than the purchased price.   Who knows, maybe Peter did me a favor when my friends put out the word that Peter's copies might have a reward involved if recovered and returned.

Though Peter was already in jail and, truth be told, I didn't care to sue him.   I figured he was in a far worse place than I could imagine, so Karma might have played a role in his judgment after all.

And by the way, to those who are interested, it is very
easy to find the difference between his books and
mine.   Being the clever guy Peter truly was, he took
precautions, I have to give credit where credit is due.
No doubt, he would not take the gamble of being
liable for plagiarism, so he removed the logo of the
publisher, and he also omitted my autobiography at
the back of the book.   So if you might happen to
have a copy of   *Love Returns Through The Portal of
Time,* that does not have a picture of me at the inside
back cover of the book, you could very well have a
rare item in your hands.   I can only hope you are
able to regain your loss when it is all said and done.

CHAPTER 3
The chivalry of the Italian…might as well be dead.

It was late in the evening.   Most of the employees had long gone.   This was the particular time that Crystal would spend pouring over the company books.   There were less interruptions and more quiet time to understand exactly how her father's company did it's business.   Quality time was spent when most had already left for the day. In fact, she hadn't realized it was well past midnight before she noticed that annoying familiar pain radiating from the base of her skull to the center of her back.   Between working at the insurance company with Bradley in the early mornings, and spending the remainder of the day in school, the evenings were all that she had left to offer. However, on this occasion it was fatigue that was getting the best of her.   She closed the books, rubbing the back of her neck.   Taking a deep breath, she sat back in the office chair that her dad had made especially for the back injury he acquired during the war.   The chair was, indeed, very comforting, but no comfort to a girl who was simply not getting enough rest.   She reached for the controls of the consol hidden just beneath the right hand rest.   With the heat turned all the way up and the messaging rollers adjusted to reach the neck muscles, Crystal closed her eyes, attempting to ease the stress that seemed to gather at the same place every time.   It wouldn't be too long before her thoughts would fall upon the direction of her life that couldn't seem more bleak

than the lonely moments spent in a darkened building
with not a soul to confide in.   Rose, her best friend
and mentor was gone.   With only a glimmer of hope
to fuel her desires, she often wondered if it was
hardly worth it.   A single tear gathered at the corner
of her eye.   It was as though Rose knew how to play
dirty in the game of life.   Knowing exactly how the
impact of loss upon Crystal's already fragile
demeanor, would go awry, Rosemary cleverly left the
strategically timed planting of seeds in the mind of
her special protégée.   I can only imagine how lonely
she must have felt.   Certainly, she didn't deserve to
be dealt the hand she was so desperately trying to
wade through.   But, thankfully, the one thread of
hope that would restore at her soul seemed to keep
vigil over her exhausted spirit.
Only, after having seen the transformation, for
myself, I never would have believed Crystal was
capable of opening her heart, much less to the idea of
a child.   But that just goes to show how much I
knew about the workings of Crystal's mind.   Seeing
her with my daughter for the first time was like
witnessing a miracle in the making.   Rosemary was,
indeed, a miracle in herself.   Having Sam work her
magic may have been a dirty trick at it's best, but it
certainly worked.   My daughter and Rosemary had
secrets that I may never come to learn, however, on
the night of Crystal's revelation with my daughter
tightly wrapped in her arms, I too was induced to
meld with the spontaneous metamorphosis.   A
sudden maternal implant took place before our very
eyes.   It wouldn't be until some time later, that I
learned what had actually transpired that night.
With a little help from Rose and Miranda, Sam was
instructed to do the mental implanting.   My little
girl has never ceased to amaze me.   With the power
of suggestion, Sam gave Crystal the gift of foresight.

Though it might have seemed, a mere second or two, it was long enough to make an indelible impression that left an indefinite life preserver deep from the spell casting mind of Sam.   She infiltrated the vision of innocence deep into the subconscious of Crystal's deepest desires.   Like a vision from God, Crystal experienced, with all her senses, what it would soon be like to have and hold her own child.

The quiet of the building offered little solace to the throb of her soul that seemed to suffer more when her mind was at rest.   The very reason, I believed, she would work herself to an exhausted frizz.   Keeping her mind busy and occupied would be the remedy from her own darkness.   After twenty minutes of daddy's, medicinal chair, Crystal was ready to face the world.   That which was not already asleep.   It was 2:00 AM.   The place was quite peaceful as she made her way through the corridor and onto the elevator.   Not a soul in sight until she reached the lobby.   The security guard would, greet her, each time, with her due respect, opening the door with the keys from his recoiling keychain and bid her a good night.   Never more personable than a, "Have a good night, ma'am." or a "Good morning, Ma'am."   As though Crystal had slipped into the shoes of her mentor, she seemed to become a young assimilation of Rosemary and her father.   And especially with the hired help.   One can only assume the guard had offered to help her to her car in the past only to be shut down by her rigid show of independence.   The door shut behind her with the chatter of rattling keys. Just another day at the office coming to a close and just a few hours before sunup.

        The parking lot was barely lit as Crystal got closer to her car.   Something was definitely amiss. The obvious contrast of dark spray paint left it's mark to be seen by all within twenty feet, from any direction.   Her, once was, white MBW had been overtly used to give warning.   The message was clear and ominous.   "Only days left, Bitch."   The paint was still wet.   The perpetrator wouldn't have had to do much surveillance to know her schedule. It couldn't have been long since the graffiti had been sprayed, though no obvious signs of kids or disgruntled employees seemed to be around.   Upon closer examination, Crystal understood exactly who was responsible.   This was not the act of kids nor an employee.   The signature vernacular of an unsuspecting foe was the only answer.   It took a lot to raise the hairs on Crystal's hide.   But this message could not have been possible, not from him. Not from a guy who was still in jail.   The car doors were still locked and the alarm hadn't been triggered. The messenger's intent was clearly intended to do one thing.   That one thing was intended to instill fear into Crystal's psyche.   If he wanted her dead, he certainly could have done that already with little effort involved.   Crystal shook her head knowing just what she was up against.   She also understood that this was just the beginning.

"Admirer of yours?"   The voice from behind her came unexpectedly.

With a rush of adrenalin and a dire hatred for the man responsible for the new paint job, Crystal reacted with cat-like reflexes.   With just an outward swing of her arm and a half pivot of her body, she pulled the Derringer from her purse, pointing the double barrel directly between his eyes.   "Fuck you."   The snarling words came quickly from between her clinched teeth.

"You must have just missed them." He said, nonchalantly using two fingers at the snout of her gun to redirect it.   He knelt to take a closer look at the paint on the front quarter panel.

If not already having pissed their pants, most guys would have felt mighty intimidated having a gun pointed at their face.   Yet, this guy didn't even flinch.   He obviously knew the peril of his situation when he pushed the gun away.   And yet, he just kept on like there wasn't a care in the world.   "The paint is still wet.   The good news is there is an all-night car wash down the street.   The bad news is, I don't have a tire pump to fill up your tires.   I could give you a lift, if you would like."

"Bob?   You're Bob, right?"   Without waiting for an answer, Crystal lowered her pistol, holstering it back in her purse that was hanging from her shoulder.   It was no accident, that gun was quick at the ready.   Crystal is no fool and quick to react. "I have an electric pump in my trunk.   Thank you though."   The trunk of the car popped open with a push of the button on her key fob.   Both Crystal and Bob knew the tires hadn't been slashed when they both noted seeing the valve stem caps lying next to each flat tire.

"Need help with that, Bella?"

Crystal was already on bended knee hooking up the pump to the valve stem ignoring the chivalry of a coworker. "My name is Crystal, Bob.   Let's keep it professional if you don't mind.   Thank you for the offer, but I've got this."   Looking as inviting as ever, she proceeded to fill each tire, dressed in her tight little skirt and heels, making sure not to scrape a knee on the pavement while keeping from spreading her legs lest she show too much lingerie.

"Prego. (You're welcome).   Auguri (Best wishes)."

"You're in America, Bob.   We speak English here."   Intolerant and unaffected by the romantic language of the Italian, Crystal was her old self, demanding of respect and self assured to a fault.

"Yes. Ma'am.   I will leave you now," Bob might have been offended by her curt response, but he didn't show it.   The smirk on his face was quite the contrast of anyone recently having been told to "fuck off."   And with an attitude equally malignant to a ravenous snake, Crystal could not have been more rude to a guy who just offered a hand.   Yet, Bob simply couldn't lose the smile that was painted across his face.   He was a proud a man with confidence to overfilling.   With his Maserati just fifty feet away the chirp of his car alarm could be heard throughout the entire parking lot.   "Tu sei donna piu bella   che io abbia mai visto. (You are the most beautiful woman I've ever seen).   Bob whispered from beneath his breath as he walked away toward his car.   Even as he climbed into the comfort of his leather seated car with all the bells and whistles money could buy, the look of total wonderment and amazement seemed to pervade.   As one last gesture of chivalry, Bob warmed up his car until Crystal inflated the last tire, packed the pump back in her trunk, and started her car.   All four tires held air, confirming the fact the culprit had merely let out the air.

Without looking back, Crystal sped off out of the parking lot and into the night.

CHAPTER 4
The reach from jail

His reputation preceded him wherever he seemed to go.   It would never fail.   Even the prisoners serving life sentences that had been incarcerated for years, came to Peter's aid offering any service he deemed necessary.   It was like he was the criminal celebrity.   Just the very opposite one might think takes place in the prison system. They had televisions with pay stations at their disposal in the cells.   Cigarettes, coffee and sometimes alcohol readily available.   And if that wasn't the shocker of the year, Peter was given preferential treatment that was kept off the books, and kept from the warden.   Special food and current magazines were just a few of the injustice he was presented with.   It was as though the man was on vacation.   He even got his long needed dental work done at the expense of, yep, you guessed it, you and me.   No doubt, a fine example of where the tax payer's money is spent.

Conjugal visits were granted without question from the very girls he cheated with on Crystal. Peter's money that was thought to be none existent was, obviously, in abundance.   One could only hope his cup would runneth over long enough to find where it was coming from.

But all the fore mentioned would not come close to the deceptive outcome of Peter's biggest plan of attack that would take place when all the cards were thought to have been played out.

He wasn't done with us.   Not by a long shot. Being in prison only gave him the protection of anonymity he needed to carry out his dirty deeds without suspicion.

Peter's favorite line of revenge would always be, "When you least expect it...I'll get yours."   I guess he thought he was a philosophical wonder.

The story of Peter's wrongdoing involving my book quickly circulated throughout the club to all our friends and associates.   Many had agreed with me, his brazen artifice was both inventive and extremely mischievous.   And yet, had it not been for my dreams I never would have suspected any plot against me.   And without the help of Bradley and my intuitive wife, never would anyone have ever known the better.   Thank goodness for gifted people.   I guess Peter didn't know what he was up against after all.   Except for the fact his plan actually worked, we at least knew of its existence and, hoped we would come up with a remedy, or reward.

"You had another of your dreams last night. Do you remember me waking you up, Baby?" Miranda's comforting fingers rubbing at the back of my neck as I sat at the edge of the bed gave me a sense of security and incredible warmth.   How did I get to be so lucky?   Her love for me gave strength enough to climb the rigors of Mount Everest and fly back on a cloud of inspiration.   She was my undying love in this life and, no doubt, countless others.   Her fingers worked vigorously at the tight muscles that seemed to have knotted up in my neck through the night.   I could feel the circulation beginning to work its way back through my back and shoulders.
"Yea, I remember.   Only too well.   Sorry, I woke you again."   The mystery of everything unknown seemed to whirl about in my mind. Trying to make sense of so many unrelenting visions plagued me in my dreams since I was a child. Making sense of them never would come easy. Thankfully, my lovely wife would, each time, manage to help me understand the intricacies of the divine, and the magic of life that would unfold each

day with unrelenting amazement, sadness and more mystery.   Even from behind me I saw the look on her face…why would I apologize for something she would expect from me?   Just the same.   "This time, I was a soldier in the military, but not like the times before."   I was gathering my thoughts, trying to remember the finer details, hoping she would be able to decipher the mystery once again.   She was patient and understanding, waiting for me to give her all the facts and more details.   "Now that Bradley is a part of our life I understood who he was.   But I didn't get the connection with him at the club."   I further explained my dream to Miranda, leaving nothing out. At story's end I turned to face my wife in hopes to gain some kind of resolve as many times before waiting for another explanation of my forgotten past. Some of my pasts would travel back centuries. Without Miranda's help and intuition I would never have been able to understand the nightmares that often kept us both up at night.   As I looked into my wife's eyes I saw something different than the times before, something of anew.

"It wasn't the past this time, Baby." she said, attempting to console me with less resolve than I had expected.   "I don't think I can help you with this one, Honey.   Your future is still unwritten.   I wish I could tell you more, but this one has yet to unfold and will only change if I attempt to interpret it as I would my own prediction."
This would mark the first time a dream-state premonition would not come to the light of understanding since my marriage to Miranda.   In fact, since our time spent together, almost all my visions were predominately of the past.   However, my judgment in people and business was never more clear.   For example, I rarely had trouble hiring help for the club inasmuch as I felt a connection of

interpretation within everyone I would meet.   In an instant I knew which kids would benefit with us and those who were not being quite honest.   With those we employed, there would always be reciprocation on both sides.   There was never a question of who should be working with us.   Whence, the tight family-like environment at the work place.

"I don't believe it.   That's a first for us.   I don't even remember the last time I had a premonition dealing with the future.   I can't help but wonder how important this might be.   All the other dreams involving Bradley had only to do with the past.   Do you think Bradley's safety might be in danger?   Do you think we should we take some sort of precautions?"   I knew I already had her answer, but it just seemed too final from somebody with such an acute understanding of her gift.

She placed her hand on my shoulder, pulling me closer, she leaned our heads together.   "You know the answer already," she sighed.   "What could I possibly tell you that you don't already know?"

"I get it.   I just hate feeling helpless.   I sometimes wonder if it is worse knowing of imminent danger or knowing of nothing at all.   We can make mistakes when not reacting properly in the face of danger all because we might have known too much, and yet, not enough."

"Bradley will be fine.   Every dream of your past has brought you closer to the truth of today. Every lifetime and every soul you encounter benefits by your healing and understanding.   You make luck happen.   Bradley will be safe.   It does no one any good to worry and stress over what has yet to reveal itself."

I knew she was right, though it took the remainder of the day to rid of the feelings that would rush me with pent-up adrenalin.

It wasn't but a single week after first meeting Bradley, the boyfriend of my newly found sister, that I realized just who he was, who Bradley was to me. Just as significant as finding my long lost sister that I was never sure I had.   I was to learn who Bradley was.   To live an entire lifetime of dreams and visions, I doubt I would ever come to know just how many lifetimes Bradley and I had shared together. In many of my pasts we were brothers.   And almost every time that we were brothers we grew up as warriors fighting side by side.   Our conquests were many, and our advantage was strong because we *were* brothers.   We were feared and undaunted. This much I know.   This much I've lived.   This much I had seen many times over.   What I could not understand, though, was why I was made to see this over anything else.   What was the purpose of so many dreams of war, bloodshed, pain and anguish? What was the message to be learned?   Is it only to know just how important my new found brother was to me?   Or did we have a war coming?   Another war to fight together?

As I recall those of my dreams, the wars were ugly, seemingly senseless and brutal.   Watching boys, some of which, too young yet to have taken a lover, giving up their lives for the sake of their country, leader or maybe religious beliefs.   Who do we have to thank for this behavior?   I suppose this is humanity at its best.   I wouldn't know.   As I awoke from each dream, Miranda fought to bring me back to the realm of reality, sometimes taking days or weeks to calm my waking days back to the present.   Like many who can't seem to shake a strange or bad dream, I too feel strangely imprinted by each experience.   Each new dream seemed to take me deeper into a challenge that I couldn't seem to free myself from.   Had it not been for the healing

energies of my Miranda, I felt I might never have
been able to come to learn many of the secrets that
came to my waking conscious.   She was my center,
my calm warm waters amid a rough sea.

There was a time when I was Jason, an all-
knowing, all seeing man of spiritual powers that
seemed to far exceed my capabilities in this lifetime.
Of course, she tells me different, my eternal optimist,
Miranda.   But I seemed to see things differently as
Mike Shane.   My purpose seemed foggy or distant
as yet.   I read aura's with impeccable accuracy and I
see only the good in others now that my life is clear
of the obstacles that hindered me when I was
younger.   But, would I even be capable of fortifying
a fail-proof way of finding her again, in the next life?
Will Rosemary bring us together then?   Is another
time capsule even necessary?   Will Miranda find
me?   Are we meant to be together for the eternal
ride?   Is it our choice?   Do any of us have a
choice?
My love tells me the past must remain in the past.
What Jason did to procure his future should have no
effect on choices made thereafter.   Such the same as
for Rosemary who knew who she would be in the
next life.   In general, I had a hard time letting fate
take the wheel.   I felt as though I must be the one to
act, not sitting idle waiting to see what happens.
Some say fate is what we make it.   I have seen both
sides of that coin, and I am not one to say which is
the proper path.   I have even staked the deck making
my will work best for me only to find later that the
path was not right for me.   Of course, if you never
bother to drop a line in the stream, don't expect to
catch a fish anytime soon.

CHAPTER 5
Family Circle

It was Rosemary's wish that, as a family, we would all gather at least once a week at a central meeting place.   Though it took nearly two months after the funeral before we would commence on such an effort, it quickly became the integral path to our healing.   Miranda and myself found it only too perfect to have us all meet at the club each week. The food and entertainment would readily be available with no chance of uncomfortable silences. Fortunately, after the first week of meeting at the club there never were any of the latter.   Especially, when Taylor was with us.   Bless her sweet soul.   I wasn't one to say that she talked too much…she simply had a lot to say, followed up by a very open opinion.   One thing was for sure, Taylor was entertaining and very sweet in a very innocent sort of manner.   I would always look forward to meeting with her and her boyfriend DJ.

Week after week, Crystal, DJ, Taylor, Bradley and Destiny met with us for dinner at the club.   As according to Rosemary's wishes we were asked to call the meetings; a Family Circle.   Each Family Circle would, first, consist of my telling a new joke from Samantha's collection.   Samantha would insist on getting feedback on each of her humorous riddles and jokes.   She had written an entire booklet of jokes, all of which were her own, and many too silly not to share.   Her joke at the very first meeting was one of her less brilliant one's. However, Crystal found her and her jokes to be adorable, and would, always, look forward to hearing what Samantha had to say.

"When is an overpass not an overpass?"   I think she thought this one up when we were traveling on the freeway.   "Give up?"   She would always insist I deliver the joke exactly as she had instructed. "An overpass is not an overpass when it is under construction."
Adorable, or perhaps even corny, we all would give a little chuckle, but it was Crystal who would always surprise me by lowering her guard just long enough to laugh and smile without any regard to her natural façade.   I believe Samantha helped to give Crystal the hope that she needed so desperately.

It was months before Crystal actually look me in the eye at our Family Circles.   I understood the effort she had to make attending each week.   I never would have faulted her for not showing up, however, she made a promise to Rosemary and she swore never to breach the contract.   Crystal would always took pride in herself and her word.   I, in fact, believe that Crystal was finally starting to warm up to the Family Circles.   Maybe even looked forward to them.   It had been four months since the initiation when Crystal brought a date along with her. Although, she never would have admitted he was her date, she brought him along, sometimes stating he was merely her escort inasmuch as real gentlemen didn't exist.   His name was Bob.   We never did ask him what his last name was.   It didn't seem important at the time as Miranda and I believed that he wasn't the Mr. Right that Rosemary had asked us to look out for.   Bob was a great guy, however. Always well dressed.   Very approachable and, each time he was able to attend, he would bring good humor and input to the table.
Of course, the main staple of our entertainment, and never fail to do so, was the bicker between Bradley and Crystal.   The two of them were an incessant

flow of insults and innuendo.   There was, irrefutably, no way to stop the banter.   No way to curtail it if you even knew how.   And there certainly wasn't anyone brave enough to get between them. Short of using a garden hose on them, I seriously doubted anything would work on their bitter rancor anyhow.   The two seemed to feed on each other.   It was like they shared some kind of symbiotic relationship of hatred for each other that kept them sane in a world of too much mundane.   If I didn't already know that the two of them were two of the most intelligent people I knew, it would not have surprised me to find out that they would stay up late nights writing down dozens of new insults and attacks for the next time they would meet.   Quite honestly, I found most of their badgering quite funny if not hilarious at times.   And each time the insults would flow with bitter cantankerous punch lines, poor Taylor would look to be in total shock.   She had never heard such talk from adults before.   The girl looked to us for assistance, and when that didn't offer any aid to the situation, she would try to intercede by trying to referee between.   And, without fail, Taylor's futile attempts at calming the rumble only added more fuel to the fire.   Each week we wondered when she would finally get it.   When would she give up trying to make them act civilized? Even DJ understood just how futile that was.   I doubt, Bradley and Crystal could have survived a day without each other.   Bradley truly needed to be expelled from the dungeons of his nerdy introverted habits.   And Crystal, simply put, well, she needed a verbal punching bag so as not to go out on the town assassinating any guy who happened to hit on her. What a pair.

CHAPTER 6
First 'Day' at work.

It was a Thursday when it first came to light, nothing special about that day.   Crystal had come to her office early that day only because school finals were over and the rest of her day was free.   She first went into her office.   She hadn't yet changed much of the decorations or furnishings since taking it over from her dad.   It actually seemed to suit her.   Upon first impression, no one would have thought it was her office, and that suited her just fine.   An appropriate sign on her door might have read; Chauvinists of the world beware, Crystal wears the pants under her tight skirt.   After setting her purse and case on her desk, and plopping herself into her daddy's chair, she immediately stepped back out into the corridor.   She seemed to marvel as to how different the place was during the day; no zombies or night stalkers lurking around, just busy minded people getting through the day's work load.   The CEO's had their own coffee room designed especially for them.   Dark walnut cabinets accented by a forest green carpet and slate tile by the stainless steel sink offered a nice warm homelike feeling. The espresso machine was stocked with dozens of different flavors for both coffee and tea.   Sweets and sandwiches were readily available in the refrigerator compliments of the company.   All in the attempt to better provide a happy and productive work environment.   With the profit margin rising by one hundred and twenty seven percent in the past four months, most would agree the java jolt didn't seem to hurt in any way, again, compliments of the new president's many ideas.

Crystal was quick to ferret her way to the largest amount of caffeine a single cup could provide.

"I was beginning to wonder if you were not a vampire."   A familiar voice startled her as she was concentrating on not spilling her brew while she stirred in the sugar.

"Excuse me?"   She didn't turn around, instantly recognizing the man behind the voice.

"Usually, you do your worst at night.   There have been exactly seven corporate meetings here during the daytime hours in the past few months all of which lasting late into the night--"

"Which means, Bob, I would have had to of travel by day to get here for those seven meetings, thus putting your theory of my being a vampire to rest."

"Unless, you were already here from the night before…" Bob slid himself between her and the machine.   Abstaining from using any Italian phrases, he poured himself a half cup of brew for himself, not bothering with any cream or sugar. "See you around, Night Stalker."

Crystal made no attempt to reply.   She continued to stir her brew as Bob seemed to have caught the corner of her eye.   As she took a sip, she found herself watching him exit the room.   He was a well dressed man in Armani and scented with her daddy's top of the line cologne.   Curious, she thought how it smelled so different on him than any of the other models used for testing.   After her sip, she stood a while continuing to stir her already melted sugar cube.

"I would hit that too if I could figure out a way to get him to look my way much less get him to speak to me.   Shit, I was beginning to wonder if he was some kind of a Eunuch or something.   So, what's your secret, sister, and is it for sale or could I just borrow it for say…twenty-seven minutes or so?"

For the first time in history of lightening speed retorts, Crystal was slow to respond as she looked to see who was addressing her.   The heavy breathing woman standing over her was also stirring her coffee that hadn't yet had any cream or sugar. The two of them found themselves leaning out of the threshold watching the male anatomy in motion.

"I'm not interested." Crystal said, with little effect on convincing the woman.

"Yeah, I thought so.   It's a serious condition with a highly technical term called 'Oh, damn, I'm a horny slut.'   Your secret is safe with me.   Don't worry about it sister, we all come down with it eventually."   The calloused vernacular seemed to have caught Crystal off guard at first.   "Pansy." She said, holding out her hand.

"Sorry."   A picture of her expression would

have been worth millions to me.

"My name," Pansy reached for Crystal's hand. "My dad named all his daughters after flowers. I got stuck with Pansy.

"No, I really am sorry." Crystal began to gain back her senses.

"Yeah well, it could have been worse. At least I didn't get stuck with Petunia or Foxglove like my little sisters, though I would have preferred my other sister's name, Jasmine. Seems so much more normal, ya know?"

"Could you imagine being named, snowball bush or bleeding heart? …Gosh I hope I didn't offend any of them. And how many sisters do you have in your garden?" said Crystal, still wondering why she was having a conversation with such a strange individual.

"I am three of nine." She answered quite nonchalantly.

"Three of nine?" The unchecked humor of the conversation seemed to have hit Crystal so unexpectedly as she chuckled uncontrollably.

Pansy shook her head in response. "We make a good baseball team."

The smile on Crystal's face that had been absent for months seemed to offer an inviting warmth. "That would be one consolation, I suppose. It's a pleasure meeting you, Pansy." Crystal offered another brief smile as she attempted to make her way back to her office. Like a shadow, keeping steady pace with Crystal's departure, Pansy stayed close and well within Crystal's personal space.

"Am I keeping you from something?" Crystal was actually attempting to be polite, which was quite difficult for her. "…like work, perhaps?" The two ladies stood at the doorway of the office with Crystal hedging towards closing the door without Pansy following.

"That would depend on you." Pansy was quick to reply.

Humoring the highly extroverted woman with a pushy presence, Crystal raised an eyebrow in question, begging for an explanation.

"If you might allow me to my desk, I could, perhaps work or…something." Pansy said, still standing too close for comfort.

In a nanosecond, Crystal recognized the situation and the possible connection that hadn't yet played a role in her business introductions. At the corner of Crystal's office was a doorway leading to a small office. The little office was scant of any personal effects like photographs or trinkets usually associated with one's office or cubicle. "The coat closet in the back…is your office?"

"Hello, again," Pansy held out her hand, once more. "I'm Pansy, your personal assistant." Pansy stood confident, vulnerable and a tad curious. She must have been at least five-feet eleven inches tall. Her attire would have been more attractive on a gazelle or giraffe, had the animal practiced better posture. It was no wonder Bob would never have noticed her. Though her nails and hair were professionally manicured, she seemed to have trouble pulling off any particular style befitting to her big bones and tall frame. She lacked any real jewelry or accessories, and her glossy black heels looked to have been purchased from a secondhand store somewhere in Victorville.

Right away, the churning wheels of her managerial concerns turned to an instant business role in Crystal's mind as she settled into her daddy's message chair. "And for the past several months, in my absence, you have been doing…what?"

Pansy held no ambiguous predispositions.

Everything she might say, without thought, was everything you would get.   She was the cover of her own book throughout.   "Working my butt off.   At least while working with Mr. Worthington I had time to get my own pedicures.   Those girls down stairs need to learn a little empathy.   The thing is, I don't have a very high pain tolerance.   There used to be a time when a 'pedi and rub' was a comfortable and relaxing event."   She was referring to the company salon.   Apparently, while assisting Crystal's dad she had enough free time to frequent the company amenities.   Or Dad insisted, making sure she didn't look like the white elephant she may have appeared to be otherwise.

Crystal stepped back allowing Pansy to enter the office.   Without hesitation, Pansy dashed into her office as if to be racing to get a mountain of work done in time for a hasty deadline.   As Crystal stood in wonder, the assistant reemerged noisily trundling a chair behind her.   At the opposite of Crystal's desk, Pansy parked her chair and abruptly flopped herself down looking as though she were an eager dog waiting for instruction.

Though Crystal wasn't much for playing catch with the help, she seemed to have found herself in a comfort zone of sorts.   "So, as my personal assistant, what exactly did Mr. Worthington have you do for him?"

Pansy took very little time to cushion her response.   "For the most part, I think I was here to look pretty.   And we both know that never materialized.   Second to that, I would sharpen pens, stock the paper dispenser in the printer and most importantly, I was put in charge of the artificial plants.   Though I'm not sure if I was supposed to water them or just watch them grow."   Without taking a breath, she continued.   "Outside of all those strenuous, back breaking duties I was really hoping to see the glamorous side of this business, that is, after all, the reason I applied for this job.   I want to meet with the rich and shameless, travel abroad with my entourage, and eat the most decadent of foods known to any antacids.   Ya know…they say it's the food that kills us?   Once somebody gets a little money in their pockets they eat the rich foods and die.

"Well long winded, girlfriend, I hadn't heard that one--"

"Of course, not *you*." snapped Pansy.

"Excuse me?"   Both eyebrows were raised in response to that one.

"Look at you, skinny as a rail.   Do you ever eat?"   Like a toy with no 'off' button, Pansy continued.   "I don't know how you do it.   I could never last a day without three squares and snacks between.   Thank goodness for my fast metabolism, I would be as big as a house otherwise.   I think--"

"I think we should test that theory."   Crystal said, curiously.

"Test?   Theory?   Ya know…I'm not very good with math or science.   I hope it isn't going to be an extensive test."

"Don't sweat it, Personal Assistant.   This test consists of the simpler equations.   I'm hungry. Would you like to have lunch with me?"

"I thought you would never ask."   Pansy's candidness was a refreshing twist from the fawning type that would normally work in such environments. She seemed to be the perfect anecdote to the very mundane that Crystal despised.

Both girls grabbed their purses and headed for the door.   "Did Mr. Worthington ever take you to lunch?"   Crystal thought she might gain a little insight as to who the private side of her dad might have been.

"The man was a machine.   He didn't eat food, I don't think.   That would be a definite 'no'."
"Yep, sounds about right."   No doubt, Crystal was a chip off the old block.
But that too, came to light, and would soon change.

CHAPTER 7
Another awakening

Another cold sweat and a rude awakening by way of a nightmare among the mystery of confusion, uncertainty and then, sudden resolution.

The dream was not of war.   It was not with Bradley at my side.   Though, this time, it was definitely of the past however, nothing like the previous ones. This dream would, finally, document the connection that I had been waiting for.   The missing puzzle piece that kept me at the edge of my seat since I was in high school was finally found and available for me to replace in perfect placement.   And now that the puzzle was complete, all the past episodes of my relationships seemed to make better sense.

I found myself amid the horrors of destitution and death by millions.   I had never seen such carnage outside of the casualties of war.   Bodies of the dead were placed into the street.   Those responsible for the clean up of dead bodies could not keep up with the work load.   The bitter acrid scent of death weighed heavy in the air.   Even with garments wrapped around the face, there was no escape from it.   Like a silent plague ebbing its way into every home of everyone I knew, the wafting fog of death crept unopposed.   Each day the death toll grew larger than the previous.   The reaper of death was indiscriminant; he took anyone in his path. Small children and babies seemed most susceptible to an immediate death.   Then the adults with strong wills and high resistance to illness would also lose the battle of their lives.   I believed, it mattered not to the reaper of death.   His path of destruction was just indiscriminant.   Those that survived would claim it was the act of the devil.   The first signs of demonic possession was the weakness of the body, followed by the inability to eat food without vomiting.   Black blotches would appear on the face and body of those soon to lose the fight of their life.   Following the black blotches, bleeding from every orifice, would confirm the imminent tale of woe.   If this attack was a battle with the devil, he never made his presence known aside from the countless screams that filled the air all through the night and day from the villagers who, no doubt, just lost another loved one. There was no refuge. No enemy to face. No man to wage war against. There was only death itself. It was a horrific episode in the history of mankind. It was a biblical nightmare, said many, only God himself could have prevented…or caused.

A month after the first onset of the plague, there were no more workers left to bring the dead out into the street for removal. The dead simply remained in the homes where they died. I don't know how my family came to survive as long as we had. My wife and kids were the lucky ones perhaps due to the fact that I had instructed them not to leave the safety of the house when I first saw the onset come to light. But, like in previous dreams, I was the healer, the one my family, friends, and neighbors looked to for remedy of the common ailments. It was my duty to help them. It was my conscience I had to contend with, had I decided not to help. Day or night, strangers and family alike would come to my door begging for assistance. The desperation in their faces was far too great to ignore. I had to try my best. I would do for them as I did for my own family. I insisted they boil water before consumption. And eat only fresh fruits and vegetables. For some, unclear reason, those who followed my instruction had a better chance of surviving the death plague, or at the very least, they managed to live a few extra days after onset. For days at a time, I was needed to leave my family. I traveled from town to town attempting to spread the word of a possible remedy. Each time my conscience would force me to help others, I would leave my family with the instructions to keep them safe.

Some of the other villagers managed to survive and helped to spread the word as well.   The mystery continued to baffle me as some still contracted the signs of the death plague, well after my treatments. It made little sense to me.   I felt as though the battle was a futile battle against a foe that was too cowardly to show his face to me.   In the dream, I felt fearless, courageous and most fortunate to be the one to share the mindset of hope and love.   But, at the same time, I was helpless with little to offer, as mothers with their dead babies still lovingly harbored in their arms, begged me to revive them.   I was not a miracle worker.   I had no Godly powers of healing. Science and medicine was in its beginning stages with little to no information on the present predicament.   The babies in every household were the first to die.   I could see the hope of many families drain away once the child had been taken by the devil.   They would give up all hope with only destitution in its place.   I could see it in their eyes. If only I could have offered more than some tiny bit of spiritual healing.

Every town was more of the same.   The death plague seemed to be global.   Why was my family so fortunate to survive?   What was so different about us?   What information was I forgetting?   After a three week revival trek through a dozen towns, I too grew week.   Fortunately, not from the death plague, but from total exhaustion.   I decided to make my way back home.   I knew I would be of no use to anyone if I, too, were to become too weak to go on.

I had a great deal of time to ponder the effects of the illness as I traveled home.   I was greatly relieved to find my children and wife still in good health when I returned.   I took the time to do some studying of our own family practice.   I soon discovered that the rosehip tea, that was the staple of our diet contained a high concentration of vitamin C. With the help of my wife and children, we would travel to the hills after dark and would gather as much of the herb as we could find.   We traveled by night to avoid the hostels that seemed to find fortune in looting and robbing those on the streets during the day.   Once we had collected a suitable amounts of plants, we created an herbal type remedy of dried tea and other plant leaves.   The dried formula was granulated and molded into a pill form and distributed throughout the town.   Those who were not too far along with the illness, quickly showed improvement, and would heal completely.   Soon the call for the remedy had traveled from town to town. I spent much of my days, thereafter, collecting and formulating the remedy for anyone who came to my door in search for help.   The remedy helped many, but not all.   The devil fought a good fight.   It surely was an uphill battle, but I kept hope close in my medicinal pouch as my savior.

It was a dreadful reality, almost too surreal to believe. The devil had found us.   My little daughter of five years of age had become too weak to help her mother in the kitchen.   She rested for a couple of days, but to no avail.   When the black blotches appeared on her body, her mother and I both knew of her fate.   I didn't want to accept the inevitable.   We kept her as comfortable as possible.   She bathed her weak little body three times a day, and her bedding was changed daily.   I knew cleanliness was an important factor with the healing process of this horrid illness. Though the harder we fought to keep her alive, the sicker she seemed to become.   She could no longer keep food in her stomach.   By the fifth day after onset, the lord had taken my child.   I instantly understood the destitution that others had experienced, displaying their grief loudly and uninhibited in the streets.   But I could not give up. I could not relent to such misery.   I had to study more, learn more, find the reason for such sporadic and undeterminable infestation.

We buried my little girl in the same field where we picked herbs from.   It was her favorite place to run free.   Not rain nor wind would keep her from enjoying her few free moments to run through the wild fields.   When she was barely three years of age I watched her grow a blissful look over her face when she witnessed her first rainfall.   We had just come back into town after a long country ride.   The horses were tired and thirsty.   She leapt from the wagon without instruction and collected the water bucket for the horses.   After filling it she placed it at the hooves of the horses.   She seemed to take pleasure in watching the horses lapping up the liquid nourishment.   As she began to laugh, we would laugh as well.   She got such pleasure from watching them.   The simple things.   It was the cutest thing ever, until we watched what happened next.   At first it was just a light sprinkle.   My little girl might have thought that the occasional drops that caught her dress might have been the splashing of the horses, but then came to realize, as the drops got bigger and more frequent, that it was simply rainfall coming down from the cloudy sky.   Something for which she had no recollection prior to that day.   Forgetting about her work with the horses, she walked mesmerized by what was happening.   She looked to the sky with absolute wonderment.   She held out her arms spread far apart.   With a blissful smile on her lips, she slowly spun her little body around and around, taking in all the drops that her little body could catch.   I had never witnessed anything more beautiful and innocent in all my life.

When I awoke from my dream I was still crying and calling out Samantha's name.   I had just buried my little girl.   I kept grabbing at Mirada's shoulders telling her that we were not as fortunate as I first thought.   "The remedy is not enough."
"It's okay now, Baby."   Miranda pulled me into her embrace.   She had already begun to read into my vision.   With tears welling up in her loving eyes, she too felt the pain I was slow to wake from. "Sam is alive and well.   It was a dream, a vision of your past."
Oh, I knew the moment she spoke the words that she was right, but it was still too painful a vision to simply whisk away.   I had no control.   I didn't care about control over my emotions.   I let the tears pour.   I cried aloud and hard while cuddled like a fetus in my wife's embrace.   Though it took several minutes to gain back my ground, I eventually found myself talking to Miranda about my past.

It was a life I never would have suspected. I was somebody I seemed to have no knowledge or recollection…until now.   "My name was Mihael.   I was French."
As always, I began to recite the events of my vision to Miranda.   It would never fail how she would be able to elaborate with far more information than I could seem to possibly extrapolate.   'I think it was the Black Plague during the fifteen hundreds or something.   My Grandfather, named Pepe, was my mentor.   I am feeling now that he was most likely, Rose in another time."   Miranda would each time make sure never to interrupt any of my recitals. Though I was awake, the recital would slide me into a trancelike state, to help me remember and recall.

"Bradley was there too, as my brother again, but this time we were not in battle.   The plague seemed to be my nemesis this time.   Oh God, how I tried so hard to heal them all.   They were so many.   Too many.   Thousands died every day."   The tears were still present in my eyes and those that were falling to the sheets.   "I lost so many, Baby."   I pulled her as close as I could knowing she would be able to read me as well.   I knew I would need her help.   I had plenty of suspicions about who was playing a part in this vision, but I needed Miranda's help to uncover the deeper meaning.   "I lost my little girl.   She was Sam's age.   I was incapable.   I couldn't do anything to save her.   A week after her death, I lost my two year-old boy as well.   I buried my children." I raucously brayed out uncontrollably with more tears rolling off my face.   "We're not supposed to outlive our kids…"   With my clutching embrace, I begged Miranda for some resolve.

"I know, Baby.   But the past has already healed and is back with us now.   Sam is well and very much an eternal kindred.   She will be with us a very long time.   Just as Bradley and Rose.   There was somebody else though?"   Hedging me to go on, Miranda always knew more than first suspected.

"My wife, Henrietta Crystaunce d'encausse." My French accent was still evident as I spoke of her to Miranda.   "She, too, died from the Black Plague. That was when all the town's people turned on me. It was not like the time of the witch burning, but a similar feeling of utter hopelessness.   I buried my entire family in a field of wild flowers.   They were as precious to me as we are now.   I can't believe I never saw them before in any of my dreams."   It took me a few minutes to gather my thoughts. Some of the facts had already begun to fade away. "She was a good woman to me…she loved to sing to us.   Though her first name was Henrietta, she preferred to be called by her middle name, Crystance. Nearly every night after dinner she would sing to us. Like most would settle around the television, now days, we listened to her voice."   I said, trying to visualize her face from the vision, but to no avail. "I can still feel her…but she is not the same person today.   She has changed…"

"Each life experience changes us to some degree.   At one point, we might be annealed by pain and misfortune, or spoiled by the windfall of fortune and luxury."   Miranda's medicinal embrace and words of wisdom kept me on track.

"I think she was a warrior at one time as well. But in this lifetime she was definitely my doting soul mate.   She watched me bury our kid's just days before she would join them.   Such a horribly painful time of misery and loss.   I can't believe I have never seen her before in any of my visions."

"Rose told me this day would finally come, Honey."
The mere drop of her name brought solace and a momentary reprieve.   "I'm not surprised you both kept this a secret from me.   The strong feelings I keep for my wife in this distant, hidden past, would easily have been severely detrimental for us all."

"Mostly for her.   Your new knowledge of her would only play with her emotions.   I can only hope the timing of your vision is truly on target as Rose had predicted."

"Certainly, I could keep from hurting her…don't you think?"   It was an honest question, though obviously misguided.

"You?   Keep from showing your feelings, Mike?   Really?   You're still wetting the sheets with tears as we speak Mr. emotional one."   She said, forcing me to take an honest look at myself.

"I suppose you're right.   So now what do we do… keep us separated again, after all this time?   How would that work?   Certainly, Rose had taken all this into account.   She has never before been off by even a second."   I thought a moment.   "Somehow, I think this is just another level for us all to get past.   There's no way to get past this now.   The damage is done.   If Crystal hasn't met Mr. Right by now, certainly, she will very soon.   It's all a matter of timing, right?"

"I don't doubt it for a moment."   Miranda began to think to herself.   "Perhaps she has yet to reveal him to us.   Perhaps she chooses to keep it private, keep him a secret from us until she could be certain."

"Are we talking about the same girl here?"   How could she have kept a secret of such magnitude.   I knew exactly who we were talking about.   I also believed that Miranda understood exactly who my wife was in that painfully horrible past life.

Miranda pulled away from my embrace taking a good look at me, but not before giving me such a look of scornful doubt.   "Crystal could keep the world a secret from you.   Now, think a moment.   You didn't even realize just how much she loved you as you went on with your life while hers was falling apart around her.   You didn't have a clue.   You are a man, you can't help it.   Don't worry about it.   It's not your fault."   She got that devious look in her eyes.   "I will need to look into this on my own.   I have a feeling she is keeping him from us."

CHAPTER   8
A week before the moment of truth

The VIP lounge was strategically located on the second floor balcony overlooking the stage and most of the club's activities.   Billy and I designed the club to our specifications keeping security and comfort in mind.   Only four other tables existed on the second floor, and they were usually reserved and booked-up four weeks in advance.   Live band entertainment, three nights a week, was crucial to my business.   The loud music, happy environment, good inexpensive food, cute girls and handsome guys were all part of the second staple to the one thing that made the business profitable; that, of course, being the sale of alcohol.   Without the sales from the bar, we probably would not have been able to stay in business.   On the weekdays when we didn't have a live band, we would have a DJ providing the dance floor with music, and we would almost always have novice performers trying their hand at comedy on live mike nights.   This was a time just before Karaoke.   The live bands we commissioned were top notch performers.   There was quite a competition to work our venue.   A few artists such

as Billy Idol, Mike and the Mechanics and Huey
Lewis and the News all got their start from working
at our club.   Through serendipity and good company
we managed to become the launching board for a lot
of eager artists struggling to make their mark in the
music industry.   I was only too happy to
accommodate and help out as best I could.   We kept
a packed club, especially on the weekends.   Many
would lineup on the sidewalk hours before we were
to open.   I had to admit, we were most certainly
blessed by such fortune.   No doubt, it didn't hurt to
have our own start with the likes of Crystal.   I know
for a fact that having Angel Flights as one of our
performers, had a lot to do with our windfall as well.
All the cards just happen to play out in the best
possible way imaginable.

By the mid eighties the top bands on the radio
were: Genesis, Van Halen, Steve Miller Band, Mr.
Mister, Peter Gabriel, Bon Jovi, Bob Segar and the
Silver Bullet Band, Inxs, The Pretenders, Heart, The
Stones, Robert Palmer, Bruce Springsteen, Don
Henley, and Lover Boy, just to name a few.   From
whom we required our bands to perform cover songs.
I would always insist on the latest in cutting edge.
Even the stage had to be top quality technology.
There was no shiny disco ball in our lighting
platform.   We had fog, strobes, oscillating spot
floods, and an assortment of sound activated color
lasers reflecting against every reflective surface of
the club.   To be able to get caught up in and lost in
the ambiance of the performances was the goal that I
felt we had accomplished.   We wanted our crowd to
have uninhibited fun.   They depended on us to
provide them with a good night, and that's what I
strived for.   Behind the scenes, there was quite a bit
of work to do, but it was well worth our efforts.
Even our security team of bouncers and spotters had

to be well practiced and vigil.   And the end result of profit and happy people proved to be a good time for all of us.

There was only one plan in mind for what she had done.   Just one reason for Rosemary having put the date on the envelope as she did.   Four years, seven months and thirteen days, from the day of her death Bradley was to open the mystery envelope. Of course, we all knew none of us would have been able to wait out such a duration of anticipation.   I don't doubt she knew that to be a virtual impossibility for any one of us to do.   And, to eventually confirm all of our suspicions, the envelope was never really intended to be opened at that specified time.   Rosemary merely intended for only one thing, and that was for Bradley to get past her loss.   She wanted him to be of sound mind when opening the envelope.   Had she put an earlier date on it, she believed he would not have waited as long as he did, thus causing a loss of understanding and a detrimental ripple effect.   Timing is everything. And knowing exactly when the envelope would be opened was what she needed from Bradley being of sound mind and, most importantly, confidence to keep an open mind.

Rose was very explicit with her instructions. Even after death, we all seemed to be reading from an instruction manual, keeping everything in order. Down to the minute we were to keep perfect cadence with Rosemary's wishes.   Our love for her was deeper than the surface could possibly reveal.   She was the lifeblood of this family.   It was her wish that we realize our family ties, and honor her wishes by meeting each week for dinner.   It was at those dinners we all grew to know, understand, and to love one another as family and not just friends.

Bradley and Destiny took an apartment together located between his law school and the office.   Though the date for marriage was never actually set in stone, they both understood it would take place when the timing was right.   Between Bradley going to college part time and overseeing the management of the insurance company, his schedule hardly left time to plan for the kind of wedding he wanted his bride to be to have, enjoy, and remember forever.   A wedding should be something to remember as a very special event.   Something *that* special would take time, money, and lots of uninterrupted planning.   However, an engagement party had taken place at the club.   Strangers and friends alike came to the party.   All who would come to the club were practically treated like family anyhow.   I was only too pleased to host the party for the two of them.   My little sister was a welcome blessing to have discovered, thanks to our beloved Rosemary.

The handoff from Crystal's tutelage to Bradley and Destiny at the insurance company went rather smoothly.   The bickering between Crystal and Bradley was held at bay just long enough for the two of them to assure a perfect harmony of exchange. Like the synchronized hand off of the baton in a relay race, the exchange of management went off without a hitch.   Destiny took instruction from Crystal, as well, without any hindrance.   Rosemary would have been so proud.   I was quite certain she was watching from her vantage point in the world of the super natural.   That old bird had everything figured out. Her ability to find my sister was my most unexpected surprise.   There wasn't a day that came to pass that one of us didn't mention her name with fondness and love.

Even though, when I was younger, I had always felt that I had a sister, the reality of Rosemary's undaunted scrutiny took some time to sink in.   I had often wondered how different our lives would have been had my mom not given her up for adoption.   I never got the chance to be the big brother, the guy enlisted to protect her.   Nor did I get the chance to know about her childhood at all.   And now, with her being a grown adult with a life of her own, I found I might never be able to know her that well.   Why would my mother do such a thing?   There had to be something deeper than the surface of what I was able to penetrate.   I had been taught that things are not always what they appear to be on the surface.   That I know and have come to realize and accept.   There was an incident long ago that had changed my stubborn way of thinking.   I, just like many others, had a set pattern, a reasoning with limited parameters.   Miranda's tutelage was a helpful resolve for opening my mind to a world of reality that existed beyond my narrow way of reasoning.

One incident that became instilled in my mind was an event that took place on the highway.   I was driving with my wife to the beach.   We were making our way to a fun-filled day in the sand.   The music on the radio was pumped as we were singing along oblivious to what was to soon be discovered. The Topanga Canyon was our usual route to the beach.   We knew the route by heart via our many trips before.   In the blink of an eye, we were abruptly passed by a driver that held no regard for the safety of others or himself as he cut us off rounding a hairpin turn.   I applied the brakes with a screeching yelp from the tires.   The seatbelt of our restraint tugged most painfully as we fishtailed into a private driveway.   Had I not already known that driveway was hiding around the turn I might have chosen a different path to escape the damage of this guy's reckless driving.   Had I chosen the other path, it, no doubt, would have been the last decision I would have ever made.   As the other driver drove through our path, he lost control of his car, side skidding into some mailboxes and a wooden fence.   His car stalled when it finally came to rest askew on the embankment.   No sooner was he able to gain back his senses from what had to be a very abrupt stop, he started his car and accelerated away.   The screech of squealing tires and the acrid smell of burning rubber was all that remained as he disappeared around the next bend.   He held absolutely no regard that we might have been hurt or worse.   I tried to shake off the adrenalin that rushed my body.   My heart was visibly pounding in my chest.   I felt the carotid arteries at my neck pulsating with unspent energy.   I looked to Miranda who seemed to be in the same state of shock.   We unlocked the seatbelts and hugged each other with a renewed passion for life. Immediately after feeling that precious love for life, my mind turned my way of thinking to bitter anger. The incident was maddening to me.   It didn't have to happen.   No act of nature, that I could see, had caused him to drive in such a manner.   I saw no reason for his actions.   Certainly, he wasn't being chased by criminals shooting guns.   I was furious that this self-centered driver would think little of our safely.   What if Samantha was with us?   I became more angered by the fact that he didn't even bother to take the time to check to make sure that we had made it through the incident unscathed.   He simply left the scene without so much as looking back.   I became furious.   Though Miranda warned me to keep my cool and not jump to any conclusions, I remained angry toward the stranger who might have killed us both.   Once we were able to settle down, we decided not to let the incident dissuade us from continuing on.

We loved going to the beach, playing in the waves and tanning our bodies in the warmth of the sun.   She reasoned we shouldn't let the incident determine our day or keep us from having our day of fun.   Certainly, she was right.   After all, anger is merely a state of mind, something we choose for ourselves.

We choose to be angry just as we choose to be happy or sad.   Surely, sad events happen that are completely out of our control, but we choose how to react to these events and how to reflect with our corresponding actions.   She reasoned with me, as she has done so many times before.   But at this particular time, I chose to be one sided.   I chose to be angry and selfish.   I *chose* to think in the only terms I allowed myself to believe.   In my mind, I selfishly reasoned that our route to the beach was the only event that lay ahead.   I allowed myself to believe that the guy must have been in a hurry to get to the beach.   And therefore was risking our lives so that he would not be late meeting up with his friends or something similar.   My rationale fed on my anger.   And my anger grew exponentially with every thought of this guy who according to my narrow thinking, had no other reason to be on road except to be heading to the beach much the same as us.   I thought, what an ass he was to think the beach might not be there when he got there.   Or what a fool to be in such a hurry.   Certainly, his friends would still be there though he might be late.   It wasn't like his friends would hate him or abandon him for being late.

Miranda knew I was still sobering over the whole event as I started the car and carefully pulled back onto the road.   We headed to the beach not saying very much.   The volume of the radio was just loud enough to be heard.   I seemed to have been checking the rear view more often than usual throughout the rest of the trip as well.   I took subtle precautions I would not have done on a normal day. We didn't feel driven to sing along to the radio the rest of the trip.   Nor did we take the time to talk about the bands that we had previously interviewed for the club.   It was as though I chose to abstain from anything that might have given me a more positive outlook for the day.   As we approached the Pacific Coast Highway, we came to the three way stop.   Our light was red.   As usual, the duration of the lights along the beach highway were rather long. As we waited for the light to turn green, Miranda and I noted the cloudless sky and the perfect weather for a day of sun tanning.   When the light finally changed, I took a second look to check for oncoming traffic from my left.   I hesitated to accelerate into traffic.   I saw the approaching car that hadn't yet come to the intersection.   The driver of the car made no attempt to stop for the red light.   As the car approached we could see it was a lady at the wheel. She appeared to be in a daze, as she drove through the intersection never slowing for the light or the possibility of cross traffic.   Had I not taken the extra precaution to wait and see if she would yield or stop as she should have, we certainly would have collided. Was this a sign?   Was it meant to be?   Did the reckless guy inadvertently save our lives?   Being t-boned by a car traveling at fifty-five miles per hour, most likely would have caved the driver's side. This was a time before side airbags.   We both thanked God for having saved our lives.   I passed it off as a sign that I wouldn't take for granted in the future.   Miranda was right to make me see things differently that what might not, at first, seem obvious. But the lesson didn't end there. I felt nearly ashamed of myself for being so narrow minded. Of course, there was no way to have known what was to come, I still felt a shame I had never experienced before.

Life guard tower number seven of Zuma Beach was our stomping ground that our friends frequented. It was sort of a territorial thing we grew to understand since high school. As we approached the parking area, we noticed an unusual number of trucks and emergency vehicles parked on the sand at the water's edge. It was an eerie sight to have witnessed. But rather than go to another beach, we chose to park and set up towels where we were used to doing so in the past. A hundred yards from where we set up our little camp I noticed the car that had cut us off in the canyon. Among the emergency vehicles, his car was amid the crowd and confusion that seemed to be congregating with a phalanges crowd making herd to see what had happened. Rather than be a rubberneck and get in the way, we stayed back and watched the incident unfold from afar. We were able to extrapolate bits and pieces of information from conversation we had overheard from people passing by. We learned that a horrible situation had taken place in the waters of the beach. Soon, we had discovered far more than we bargained for. The incident unfolded with a tragic accident involving a young girl of sixteen. Apparently, she was body surfing with her boyfriend when she was stung by a jellyfish. Thanks to the quick thinking of her boyfriend, he pulled her from the crashing waves and brought her to the safety of the beach. Unfortunately, the lifeguards nor the paramedics who first responded were able to revive the young girl from what turned out to be a fatal allergic reaction.

They worked on her for nearly an hour administrating CPR but to no avail.   Her throat had closed precluding any lifesaving attempts known to the first responders.   The poor young girl died within minutes of the first signs of Anaphylactic shock.   I felt so sad for the young girl and her frightened boyfriend who was showing obvious signs of near hysterics.   It was a familiar loss to jar my own memory of loss.   I had lost my girlfriend, Diane at the approximate age.   The memory of such a loss impacted me with a heavy feeling of hopelessness. The renewed memory of my own loss hit me with a very unsavory mood change.   The day was turning out to be the strangest to be sure.   I had gone from irrefutable anger, to passionately grateful when driving to the beach.   And then, sorrow seemed to be the culmination, or so I thought would be the final culmination.   Nothing could have prepared me for the final conclusion that would slap me upside the face like a two-by-four lifted and projected by way of a tornado.   I could not believe what I came to learn that sad day.   What transpired would haunt me the rest of my life.   We soon discovered why that crazy driver was in such a hurry in the canyon, and why he had parked his car on the beach as he did.   The driver was the father of the young girl who had died on the beach.   Making matters more remorseful was the fact that the woman who nearly broadsided us was the mother of the young girl racing to be at her daughter's side through the final moments of her young life.   Unfortunately, neither parent got the chance to say goodbye to their young daughter.

Would I have reacted any different than either of those panicked parents?   I honestly don't know. We all tend to throw caution to the wind when it comes to our children.   I am guilty of speeding mine to the hospital on a couple of occasions.   I don't

*deny it.   Would I drive as reckless?   I don't think
so, but I preferred not to think about it.   We all tend
to think it could never happen to us.   Many are not
so fortunate.   I learned a worthy lesson that day.
So I ask myself the million dollar question; did my
mom have good reason for her actions?*

Though anger, hatred, and guilt have no place
in the life of a positive mind, I could not help but
harbor some measure of animosity.   It just seemed
so unfair.   One consolation, however, was knowing
that Destiny was in good hands with Bradley.   She
was raised with adequate and a sound wellbeing.
And though Bradley felt somewhat awkward around
me, I knew someday we would become much closer.
So many times I wanted to tell him of our past lives
together as brothers, but the timing never seemed to
mesh appropriately, and he had so much on his plate
already, I figured there would be time for such
awakenings.   The dregs of knowing of our past
would sometimes hamper the honesty of our present.
For example, I knew that Millie was born blind in our
previous life.   And in the short few months of being
together with my sister both Miranda and I
recognized the signs already prevalent with Destiny's
difficulty in finding the proper pair of eye-glasses.
It seemed each week she was having to acquire a
stronger lens.   I could not imagine how difficult it
must have been for her always struggling to see and
still carry on with business.   She was a patient one
though.   She seemed to take everything in stride.

One time, at the club, with the soft lighting,
Destiny seemed to be having difficulties reading the
menu.   Though she made an attempt to clean the
lenses of her glasses, the effort, evidently, made no
difference.   But instead of making any fuss over the
situation and calling any attention to herself, she
quietly folded the menu and pushed it to the side

while cuddling up to Bradley who shared his menu with her.   He caught on in an instant asking her what she might prefer; chicken, pork, fish or red meat as he would, most times choose.   The two worked so well together, like a well versed sports team anticipating the other's every move and emotion.   I suppose, if I didn't already have such a wonderful family of my own, I might have been jealous…or bitter like Crystal was to Bradley.   Destiny and Bradley were extremely easy to read, which made things even worse for Bradley when Crystal was around.   The poor guy couldn't think fast enough to keep up with her piss and vinegar.   It nearly seemed that the moment Bradley would get an erection Crystal would instinctively hear it, even from across the room, it didn't matter where he might be hiding out with my sister.   "Hose those two off," or "Get a room." Seemed to be the normal reaction from Crystal.   Fortunately, Bradley is a good sport.   For the most part, we recognize this as a good partnership.

On Oldies But Goodies Night at the club, which also fell on one of our Family Circle Nights, Crystal shocked us all by abruptly heading to the stage without saying a word to any of us.   I doubt even Bob knew what she was up to as he helped her to her feet.   "I will be right back." was all she said. Crystal proceeded to make her way down the stairs and to the stage.   She spoke with the guys of the band for a brief moment followed by her taking the lead on the stage.   Standing before the audience with the mike in hand, she simply introduced herself as Crystal, and waited for the band to strike the first note.   The hustle of the club was always loud and sometimes rather noisy.   As the band was playing, some would be dancing, others talking, laughing and caring on with conversation without a care in the world.   When Crystal introduced herself, such was the same as usual, laughter from couples sharing their privy moments, dishes clattering in the kitchen, and the normal scuffling of chairs dragging along the hardwood floor.   Even after the first five notes of Crystal's chosen song played out, for the most part, she was ignored and unnoticed by the crowd.   And then, it happened.   Like someone had shot off a cannon.   Crystal opened up with her first verse.   In an instant, the club fell quiet.   Her amazing voice cut through the air swiftly and bold.   All business came to a crashing halt.   The kitchen silenced as each of the cooks and help emerged from the back. One by one, they filed out to see who was singing on stage.   The cocktail waitresses all stopped and stood in tribute.   Every patron in the building watched, hanging on to every note that girl sang.   She was nothing less than purely amazing.   Her voice was powerful and as clear and primed as we had ever heard her to be.   She sang a song I had never heard her sing before.   Quite frankly, I had never heard her sing a song from the oldies collection before, much less a song as poignant.   Those who were previously dancing stood in, what looked like, a trancelike state just staring in awe.   The words of the song cut it's path like a heated knife through butter.   She sang Connie Francis' Where the Boys Are.   If you have never heard this song before, I urge you to do so now.

       With most of us knowing of her painstaking courage and losses, there wasn't a dry eye at our table.   She amazed us all, so unexpectedly. Nothing was rehearsed or staged.   And then, upon the very last note of the song she chose to sing, she acted as if she had just scratched an itch or smoked one of her cancer sticks.   She replaced the mike back on the stand and thanked us all for our time and stepped off the stage like nothing had ever happened. As she made her way up the stairs and back to our table the applause continued until she took her place seated at the table.   The band reintroduced her encouraging more applause.   Yet, she took no notice.   Public relations seemed to be unimportant and the last thing on her mind.

Bob, who had attended the Family Circle at this particular time, stood to aid her way back to the seat next to him.   He was a gentleman to Crystal at every opportunity.   No doubt, he was quite fond of her. We all could see that quite plainly.

Seated at our table were Bob, Taylor and DJ, my sister and Bradley and Miranda and me.

In his baritone voice, Bob placed her cloth napkin in her lap whispering just loud enough for us all to here, "You are so sexy, Bella."

Unable to clear her throat fast enough, Taylor spoke out, "You are a god, Crystal!   The look of absolute amazement could not possibly have been removed from her face, not even with a recently fueled blowtorch at point blank range.

"And you are adorable, thank you, Taylor."

"You, I'm afraid," looking directly at Brad and pointing a finger, she continued, "you're still a geek all day."   Spoken like the Crystal we all learned to love and adore.

"I love you too, Crystal."   Bradley would, often, resort to the ineffective reverse psychology technique.

"Of course you do, Dork."

Bob had attended a couple of our meetings prior to this day, but this was the first that he had actually voluntarily participated in deeper conversation.   I figured he needed to get to know us better first.

"How do you put up with her?"   While leaning forward to see around Crystal, Bob looked directly at Bradley earnestly wondering what the deal was between the two of them.

"I keep a flask in my pocket." Brad said, tapping at his suit jacket.

"Ah, the medicinal remedy." Bob nodded. "Let me guess.   You're a whiskey man, or perhaps brandy?"

"No…Holy water."   Brad announced.

That one had me in stitches.   When Bradley would finally put his retorts in order, he did rather well against Crystal's repertoire of insults.   I rather enjoyed listening to the two of them.   The volleys between them would sometimes go on for several minutes.   Our ribs and cheeks would ache with laughter.   If only I had gotten into the habit of carrying a note pad with me, I might have written a book about all this scintillating madness.

Taylor was still trying to attempt to gather her thoughts and make some kind of impression on Crystal, "No, I meant what I said.   You are fantastic. I have never heard anything so beautiful in my life. You have a phenomenal voice…my God, I love you…" boasted Taylor, with her hands folded against her chest.   "No really, I'm in love with you and that voice of yours."

"Aren't we all." said Bob, showing a side of him he would normally keep hidden from us.

"Amen to that."   Destiny said, raising a glass of red wine.   Even Bradley chimed in with the toast of clanking glasses.   The man seemed to hold no animosity toward her, even after all the hostility.

Still shaking her head in a fog of astonishment, Taylor continued with a worthy impromptu interview "Why aren't you still singing? If I had a voice like that…   What could possibly be keeping you from continuing with such a glamorous career?   You obviously haven't lost your voice like the tabloids are claiming."

Much less reluctant to answer as she had been in the past, Crystal cast a distant smile that I could read from a mile away.   "It's not the voice or the money that keeps me from singing, Sweetie." Followed by a deep sign, Crystal explained more than her usual persona.   "I lost the drive.   And…I'm a selfish person who has developed other needs." Crystal tugged at her tennis bracelet while trying to find the words, seemingly, hoping to put Taylor's lust for fame to rest.   "The public doesn't deserve to put up with me.   I failed too many people to make things right."

With her arm pointing to the stage Taylor nearly jumped out of her seat, "With a performance like that I am quite sure the *public* will forgive you…and screw those who don't.   They want y--"

"I would have to want it too, Taylor." said Crystal, with a snap to her response.

"Than what was that?"   Taylor pointed to the stage once more.

"That was our Crystal granting us one last gift."   I felt the need to rescue Crystal from the assault of tabloid drama.   "Sort of a peace offering." Though it was more than that judging by the choice of song she chose, I could clearly see that Crystal had certainly and graciously accomplished another rite of passage.

Crystal looked to me with a calm in her brown eyes and a look of contentment and an unconditional agreement, "I've got this, Mike.   It's okay."   Turning to Taylor, Crystal put it all on the table devoid of any vanity, pride or ego.   She spoke slowly and assuredly with a voice that was soft as silk,   "You see, Taylor, I am in love with a man named Mike Shane.   However, that man was never meant to be with me--"

"Oh my."   Taylor fell back in her seat looking confused with wide eyes.

"Exactly," Crystal confessed.   "That very special man was meant to be with Miranda.   I would want nothing less for them than to be happy and together.   And had it not been for Miranda we might never have had that very special little girl named Samantha…who has opened my eyes to an entirely new world."   Still tugging at her bracelet, she didn't need to search far for the words.   "And I want you all to know that I am aware that I have made some poor choices in the past.   I can't say that I regret them…we wouldn't be here together if any one thing was different.   Rose has brought me into the light of passage.   We all know how she saved my life.   I wear this bracelet that Rose had designed for me with pride and, until now, as an unspoken promise.   Each diamond represents the first thirty days of my sobriety.   I will remain an alcoholic until the day I die.   And I will fight to survive each sober day, one day at a time for the rest of my life.   Though the path of our destiny isn't always clear to us, I understand that I must reap where I have sown until my righteous path is revealed.   Just know and understand that I love and appreciate all of you, as family…well, except for Bradley.   I simply can't afford to go back to a life that has nothing but hard memories.   And now I have promises to fulfill to each of you as well." solemnly, she leaned against Bob's shoulder who, graciously, received her in his embrace.

The last ditch effort towards levity, by mentioning Bradley, did little as Taylor was the first to cry, silencing any more of her inquiries and natural curiosities.   The sorrow-filled moment of silence

weighed heavily on all of us.   Finally, it all seemed
to make perfect sense to Taylor.   Prior to this
awakening, she had all the pieces to the puzzle, but
hadn't the understanding to put it all together.
Miranda and Destiny were next to show their
unbridled tears.

"Thank you," she whispered to Bob as she
tucked herself deeper into his harbor.   Her distant
stare seemed to carry her away to a distant privy
place of contentment.

"Think of me as your beast of burden."   Bob
whispered to Crystal.

"Whence the name B o b."   Bradley said
under his breath.   My brother of a past life was,
indeed, the king of acronyms, and, perhaps, of bad
timing as well.

The silence at our table was suddenly broken
by the cocktail waitress requesting drinks to be
refreshed.

Bob was the first to ask Crystal what she
desired.

Whispering, she suggested, "The usual."
She placed her hand on Bob's leg.   It couldn't have
been easy for him to hear her say such words if he
truly had the feelings for her, we all seemed to
perceive as quite obvious.

Undaunted by what was in the past, Bob
never took his eyes from Crystal's as he ordered,
"For the lady, a tonic with a wedge of lime.   For
myself, a bitter sweet Scotch, easy on the eyes."   If
Bob had a middle name, it probably would have been
suave or debonair, of which, he, no doubt, was the
very epitome.

"We have Chivas Regal if that's acceptable."

Keeping his eyes steady on Crystal, Bob
replied, "It couldn't be regal enough to compare to
such beauty, but that will do just fine."

Crystal accepted his flattery, in return, offering him her patented smirk and a tender kiss on the cheek.

That was the moment Miranda and I recognized the signs to watch for, however, our feverish curiosity nagged at us, wondering if he was the one.   He fit all the descriptions that Rosemary had defined for us, yet his name and occupation didn't fit at all.   We were informed that Mr. Right would be an Italian who was a CEO working with Crystal at her dad's company.   But, Bob was a traveling salesman who we were told came from a rich family living in Calabasas, California.

As the rest of us ordered drinks, I watched Crystal and Bob whispering privately.   The signs of admiration that were evident in her eyes, showed a past that had been long abandoned.   Could he be the one?

"So, Bradley, I understand that you are going to law school now.   How's that going?"   DJ started conversation pulling us out of the state of depletion and depression.

"I only just started a few weeks ago. Though it seems to be quite interesting.   I think it will come in handy at the firm." Bradley took to calling the insurance company *the firm.*   Perhaps that was lawyer lingo.   "And you, still working with computer programming?"

"Yea, I should be getting my associate's by the end of this semester."

"That's fantastic."   Destiny raised her glass for another toast.   I think my little sister may have had a hidden passion to drink.   "Congrats to DJ. I'm sure I speak for all of us when I say we are all very proud of you."   She spoke to him like a big sister, always keeping an eye on him and offering just rewards.

"Perhaps, when you two get the chance and make the time, we might be able to meet and work out a computer filing system for my company.   My father's antiquated system needs to be brought up to date."   Never before had Crystal mentioned business at the table of our Family Circle.   It must have been important enough to benefit all involved.

Both boys looked to each other, shrugging shoulders, agreed without reservation.   "Sure. Sounds like a date."

"Good.   Whatever the outcome, I want you to know that I will compensate the both of you for your time."

DJ and Bradley both spoke affirmatively. "It's not necessary."

"Yes it is.   Don't ever sell yourselves short. Demand payment for your expertise or people might think you the fool, or worse, try to take advantage of you."   The words eerily sounded identical to the vernacular most commonly heard from Rosemary.

"Okay, you got it Crystal." Obliged DJ, showing no further contest.

Still attempting to wipe the fog of confusion from her mental capacities and the sadness she held out for Crystal, Taylor responded, "Well, I couldn't be more proud of him.   He is the best."   She clutched at his arm as she smiled gleefully at him.

"You must let us know when you have your certificate in hand so we can post it out in the open and help you celebrate here at the club, if that's okay with you, DJ?"   I said, hoping to have reason for another big club party.

"You bet, we wouldn't miss it for the world. Maybe you could book a famous band for the party." Taylor impulsively answered for DJ. "Oh, that might have sounded bad, huh?"   Taylor had a habit of speaking aloud with little forethought.   "I'm sorry

Crystal, I didn't mean to offend you."

Crystal's smile was genial and somewhat curious to us.   With each day passing we could see her temperament becoming slightly softer, and her personality a bit more amicable. "I'm not offended, Honey."   Crystal seemed to be formulating some kind of plan.   "Taylor, are you the kind of person who is interested in, and would like to *be* in the limelight?   Or do you prefer to *meet* with those in the lime light?"

Taylor thought a moment.   "I hadn't given it much thought, but I think I just want to meet the stars and learn all about them.   Besides, I don't have the kind of talent needed to *be* famous.   Why do you ask?"

I was wondering the same thing.   *Why would she ask that?*

"Talent is a simple matter of perspective. You seem to have a penchant for the inquiring minds. And from what I can tell, you're certainly not a shy young lady.   You speak what's on your mind, and that could work in your favor.   Do you like to travel?"

"I don't know, really, I never have."   Taylor looked to DJ for approval.   And from what I could see, DJ didn't seem to mind, however, still hesitant with a bit of reservation not knowing what the discussion was leading to.

"Are you tied down to any obligations at this time?   Could you be available right away?"   Bob was quick at the ready, helping Crystal to her feet as she continued to question Taylor.

"I would have to make arrangements with Grandma Tilly, but I doubt she would mind having to replace me.   That is to say…if it meant something important for me, I suppose."

Crystal offered her sly smirk, "I have a friend

that you might be interested in meeting.   Maybe we *can* make this something important for you.”

“Oh, do tell…rich and famous, a movie star or a rock star?   A girl, a guy?”   Taylor scoped the club, panning quickly through the crowd, bobbing and weaving her head hoping to catch a glimpse of a movie star, a big producer or director.   “Is she here now?”   She said, jumping from her seat with a burst of blissful energy.

“Whoa, slow your horses, girlfriend.” Crystal motioned for her to sit and calm herself.   “I spotted *him* here earlier, I suppose he might still be. He’s not a movie star.   He’s more like the behind the scenes kind of guy.   Give me a moment to speak with him and I will be back.”   With that, Crystal was off again, no doubt, supplying us with another of her unsuspecting surprises.

“Well, aren’t you the lucky girl?”   I felt the impulse to comment.   Not only had Crystal turned friendly, but helpful as well.   I too, began to wonder what she had in store for Taylor.

“I guess so.”   Taylor replied, excitedly. “Who do you think she’s talking about?”

“I have no idea.   She has lots of friends and connections.   It could be anyone.   I, for one, am looking forward to seeing what she has up her sleeve as well.   I think she is quite taken by you.   I wouldn’t take her favors lightly, either.   She is not one to give without certain provocation.”

“And she called me girlfriend.”   Taylor smugly added.

“That she did, Taylor.” Miranda confirmed, offering a warm smile.

CHAPTER 9
Getting to know Pansy

"Your car or mine?"   Pansy asked, graciously.

"I'll save you the gas.   My treat."   Crystal led the way out of the building and into the parking lot.   There could not have been more contrast between the two of them.   Crystal's designer clothes, perfect make-up and daddy's finest perfume couldn't cover up the lack of class and style that emanated from Pansy's dizzying choice of wardrobe. Since the day Crystal found the graffiti on her car, she made a habit of parking her car closer to the building and in her own designated spot.   The only reason she hadn't parked her car in her own spot on the day of the paint job was because someone had taken liberties and decided an empty parking spot so close to the building shouldn't go to waste. Unfortunately for that guy, Crystal had his car towed to the impound upon her arrival that day.

Though her effort to improve her safety may have seemed appropriate enough, it obviously didn't hamper the efforts of the one trying to put the fear of God into her daily routine.   Sitting in her parking spot safe and sound was her freshly washed and waxed BMW showing no sign of trauma or fresh graffiti.   Instead, she found the simplicity of an envelope pressed beneath her wiper blade.   Obvious to her, the message was from the same person as before.   Scrolled across the envelope with the same penmanship, Crystal recognized the calling card, leaving the exact same message.

"I saw that."   Pansy announced.   "Bitch, huh?   I'm betting the impound fees were more than Mr. Parker had anticipated."

Crystal was very good at hiding her emotions,

"Ahhh.   A word of advice, don't fucking park in my spot and there won't be any costly impound fees."

"You got that right, sister."   Pansy said, offering accolades in her tone.   "Shouldn't we have a look-see?   Read what he had to say?   Of course, I don't suppose he would be asking you out. Although he is kind of cute."

Crystal offered a weak chuckle as they climbed into the car.   She tucked the envelope snugly into her purse choosing to seek the contents later.   "Not interested in what he would have to say, really. Like I said, I'm hungry.   And when I get hungry I get angry.   You wouldn't like me when I get angry."

"Don't I know it.   We're from the same stock, sister.   I can tell."

"That being said," Crystal turned the key. "Thank goodness for vegans and the people of P. E. T. A."

"Aside from the obvious bush eaters, why should *we* be grateful for those who prefer to eat rabbit food?"

"For the same reason I am thankful for the non smokers."   She put the car in gear, revved the engine and pulled from the lot.   "More smokes and juicy red meat for the rest of us."

"Point taken.   I couldn't agree more." Pansy said, adding her own clever twist on the acronym. "P.E.T.A.; People eating tasty animals."

"Perhaps we are more alike than I first thought, Pansy.   We are going to get along just splendidly, *sister*."

The two went to lunch at the nearest steakhouse.   They shared stories, company secrets and good wholesome conversation.   This would be the first time Crystal had actually enjoyed herself outside the company of Rosemary and those of us at the Club.   Finding Pansy was good for her.   It allowed her to escape from her own mind for awhile.   Over the next several weeks the two spent much time together.   Some of which was applied to the business and most was fortifying a closer friendship.   Mr. Worthington chose well.   Pansy was innovative and clever in the office as she was a comic and personal confidant to Crystal.   They made a good team.   And as Bradley required less of Crystal's time at the insurance company, the more time she was able to spend working her father's business with Pansy as her personal assistant.   Though, it didn't take long before Crystal had her fill of Pansy's shortcomings in the arena of fashion, good taste and style.   Working with a company that devotes all its invested energies towards the finest fragrances and cosmetics the industry could possibly afford required very particular stringent protocol in the fashion world.   Something Pansy seriously lacked.   It is one thing to pay big money for an expensive outfit.   But it is an entirely different turn of events to understand just how to put together a perfect style with exquisite fashion sense.   Crystal was the epitome of the latter.   It was bred into her from birth and continued to develop in her lifeblood.   As she lived and breathed, the Ritz of name brands made all the difference in her very being and trade.

     Befitting the proper role in what Crystal would call a duty to the trade, she took Pansy on an emergency shopping spree.   They never made it back to the office that day.   No sooner were they done with lunch, Crystal decided she needed to extinguish an urge to help a companion in dire need of a complete makeover.   For Pansy, it was a dream come true, to have been granted the privilege of such an honor provided by the very queen she worshiped.

First on the list of urgency was to get Pansy to Rodeo Drive in Beverly Hills as soon as possible.   Unlike Sears and JC Penny, where Pansy would frequent, the boutiques of Crystal's preference where like nothing Pansy would have expected.   At each location, the help already knew of Crystal's expensive taste and reputation, and would work with her accordingly. From the moment the two came in the door they were received by a personal assistant who would stay with them through to the final sale.   Pansy was fitted with the finest.   I knew exactly how she must have felt being pampered by such luxury and supply.   I, too, was once in her shoes when Crystal took such pleasure in outfitting me, in what seemed like a lifetime earlier.   The woman had an eye for perfection.

With the combination of no clocks on the walls, the complimentary danish, coffee, and all the special attention, the girls fell deeply into the thralldom of blissful shopping.   They must have hit three stores before the conversation finally turned from the business section to the personals.

The sales clerk handed Pansy a stunning red dress from the Coco Chanel rack.   "So what's the story with you and the Eunuch?"   Since the very first, Pansy was dying to know about any dirt that might exist between them.   "You're the only one in the entire company to have piqued his interest in girls, and you shut him down like a leaky faucet." Pansy tugged and wrestled with the zipper on the dress almost seeming frenzied and rushed to be offered such an expensive design.   "The way I figure it, we are dealing with one of two scenarios here.   You're either a lesbian, or you recently got your heart torn out and served to you on a steely, cold platter.   Though I doubt I'm your type, I'm willing to try just about anything, Sweetie."

Crystal launched a sidelong glance stout worthy of heterosexuals.

"Or not!   I just thought I'd throw that out there.   Just in case there was any brown nosing to be done in the name of the business and job security, of course."

Crystal fell victim to another of her long glassy stares.   All the lights in the house were on, but nobody appeared to be home.

"HELLO…so, that's how it is…give me his name.   I'll punch his clock, and then we can go celebrate by having you buy me another pair of shoes, girlfriend."   Pansy said, teasingly serious.

"No, that won't be necessary.   I'm perfectly capable of punching clocks on my own should the need arise."   Crystal said, not readily eager to reveal any shattered romance stories.

"Not willing to spill you're guts to me, yet?" Pansy thought to humor her using a German accent. "You know, we have vays of making you talk, Fraulien."

Crystal quickly responded mimicking the same accent, "And I have vays of making das nosey ones unemployed."

"Your point well taken, boss."   Pansy was so busy trying to slip herself into a slinky one-piece dress she hadn't noticed, Crystal was still sobering over the discussion.   "Well, you know what they say?   It's better to have loved and lost, than never to have loved at all."   Pansy was quite impressed with what she was seeing in the mirror.   "Or, did I say that back wards?"   Pansy reiterated.   "It's never too late to have loved them all, than lost at love that could have been better.   Yep, that's how it goes.   I can never seem to remember those silly phrases."

Crystal's weak chuckle was only a reflexive response to what was only background babble to her ears.

"Damn, I look good."   Pansy turned in the mirror this way than that, never taking her eyes from the fit that accentuated her derriere.   She gathered up her thick red hair, twirling it into a bun at the back of her head.   As she struck a pose, she fell awestruck.   "Oh, ask me for my phone number."

"Ok, I'll bite."   Crystal said, willing to play along.   "Hello, gorgeous.   That's quite a dress you got there, Missy.   How about you give me your phone number and I help you out of that dress, say…at my place, eight sharp."   Crystal said, sounding like the many who have tried their luck with her.

Pansy was only too happy to deliver her line, "I don't date gay Italians.   Besides, do I look like I would have a fucking pencil?"   Pansy posed proudly revealing the tightness of her, wraparound, designer dress.

"You really think he's all that?"   Crystal inquired.

"Gee, I haven't a clue.   Who you are talking about, again?"   Her playful aristocratic attitude fit as tightly as the dress.   Pansy continued to turn to every possible view of her butt.

"He's a pompous ass.   Why would you want to get involved with that?"   Crystal said, fighting with her own emotions.

"Trick question, right?   Because he's a sexy pompous ass...has a sexy pompous ass, or which ever.   And it's not *me* who is interested.   I have eyes.   I can see.   Anyone within striking distance could see you had marked him for yourself."

Crystal hadn't realized she might have tipped her hand.   But more to the point was the fact that Crystal, herself, hadn't yet realized her attraction to Bob.   Could it be possible for Crystal to finally show an interest in another relationship? "I'm not ready for a relationship, Pansy. You got this all wrong."

"Yeah, okay, whatever you say, boss. Your secret is safe with me. How long has it been since your last go around anyhow? Months, a year or two?" Pansy took a moment to read the signs. "More? Three, four? Holy shit, woman." Pansy read right through the light brown eyes that filled glassy and lonesome. "Oh, sweetie, I had no idea." Pansy took a seat next to Crystal on the viewing couch. "This is far more tragic than I could have thought. Here you are fixing me up like your very own dress up Barbie doll, playing Santa Clause, all the while, you are dying from a decade old case of sex deprivation. This won't do. We need to get you laid, stat."

"No, we don't." Crystal snapped.

"Are you sure? I was kinda hoping to do the town with you and this gorgeous snake skin."
Pansy said, giving sad puppy eyes.

"You and that gorgeous dress will do fine on the town without me." Crystal was surely not to be swayed. " I have work calling my name. Perhaps another time."

Pansy hooked her pinky with Crystal's, "Rain check, can't be taken back." It was the very same hand gesture that Samantha would often make when imposing promises.

"I promise." said Crystal through a foggy haze that brought her immediately to the memory of a day she shared with Samantha.

It was a day while I was away at the club working on more modifications to the stage effects. Miranda had invited the girls over for a little impromptu get together. Unbeknown to Crystal, the subterfuge had worked perfectly, getting Crystal to come to the house so that Samantha would have a partner to play with.   Rosemary and Samantha had played many games of Duck Hunt together on her Nintendo console.   However, Crystal was surprised to find that Samantha was also quite fond of playing Checkers.   Crystal was already well practiced at shooting things.   Choosing to steer clear from games of violence, Crystal chose checkers.   Game after game, Samantha became more of a challenge.   The two played together like sisters.   It wasn't long before the two chose to play other games of mental strategy.   Each game would leave Crystal marveling at how intelligent this little girl of six actually was. It didn't surprise her to find that Samantha had a huge library of mental challenges to play on that console.

After streaming from one game to another, Samantha challenged Crystal to a few of her favorite riddles.   On the chalkboard of her bedroom wall, Samantha wrote the phrase; Madam, I'm Adam. She then asked what was the significance of the phrase.   When Crystal gave up, Samantha wrote on the chalkboard another short phrase, stating that this phrase held the exact same significance.   Step on no pets.   Again, Crystal had trouble figuring out what the significance might have been.   Immediately, Samantha would laugh and pride herself with tricking another adult.   She explained to Crystal how easy the answer was, "Both are palindromes, phrases spelled backwards the same as foreword."

"Well, aren't you the most clever little girl." No doubt, it had been quite awhile since the last time she might have played games with anyone.   With few game type resources of her own to rely on, Crystal turned to tongue twisters.   Having studied music and worked hours of voice and singing training, Crystal was well versed in the areas of verbal tasks and challenges.   "Well, can you say, Sam shaved seven shy sheep?"

As Samantha made her best attempt, she stumbled a tad and laughed at herself with each attempt.   "I have one for you," Samantha boasted; A skunk sat on a stump.   The stump thunk the skunk stunk.   The skunk thunk the skunk stunk."   Though she herself had a bit of trouble saying the riddle, Samantha felt assured she would be able to fluster Crystal's tongue.

Crystal repeated the riddle flawlessly and very rapidly.

Amazed, Samantha insisted she say it again even faster.

And Crystal obliged, flawlessly repeating the twister with, seemingly, little effort.

"Wow, that was fast.   You are good.   Do you know anymore of those?"   Samantha was enthralled by such an ability that Crystal came by naturally.

"Okay, last one; A tutor who tooted a flute tried to tutor two tooters to toot.   Said the two to their tutor, is it harder to toot or to tutor two tooters to toot?"

Samantha gave it a brief attempt, failing to laughter and some incidental flatulence.   The two began to laugh as Samantha would continue to toot as well.   According to Miranda, the two were in near hysterics when she came into the room to see what the commotion was all about and what was so funny. Tears were streaming down Crystals face as she tried to gain back her composure.   Though I would have loved to have seen such an event, no doubt, my presences probably would have tainted the event.

"Tongue twisters Mommy.   Crystal is great at it."

"But it's all over now with no repeats."

Crystal stood up from the little child couch, straightened her skirt and hair, and gave Samantha an endearing hug.   Each time the two were together, it would nearly bring Crystal to tears.   The idea of having to part from my daughter, or the fact that, one day, Crystal would be fortunate enough to have a child of her own.   Who knew what the tears were for?   Only my little girl would have insight enough to know.

"Can we do this again sometime?"   Prattled little Samantha with her yearning eyes.

"I don't see why not."

"Promise?"   Instantly, Samantha hooked Crystal's pinky with her own, insisting she make the promise.   "Can't be taken back."

"I promise."   Crystal agreed.

CHAPTER 10
Pansy's awakening

Pansy and Crystal seemed to hit it off from the start.   One might never know what chemistry it takes to attract friends but, in Pansy's case, she was quick of wit and horny as hell.   Perhaps the combination fit well within the parameters of Crystal's current superficial needs.   Or as Miranda would simply say, it's a girl thing.   *And I leave it at that.*

The day after Pansy's make over, was an awakening of monumental proportions.   She wore her favorite outfit adorned with all the accessories Crystal had outfitted with her.   Her hair had been cut, styled and colored to enhance its beauty.   She had been given new ideas on how to use a better line of makeup to pronounce the seductive curves of her face.   Her eyes were a resplendent blue, enhanced by the colors used by the makeup artist, trained to know what works to bring out the finest of natural beauty.   Pansy was unrecognizable.   Her beauty surpassed her own expectations tenfold.   The awkward walking Giraffe who once graced the halls of that perfume and make up company had vanished overnight.   Her physical transformational makeover manifested a change in her mental status as well. The confidence in her walk developed exponentially with each addition to her makeover.   She witnessed herself bloom in the reflection of the mirror that changed her life that very magical day.   Her first day back at work attracted every pair of eyes she had ever wished for.   Heads turned from every office she would pass.   And pass them she did, sometimes more than once, just for effect.   At times, she would be mistaken for a new employee.   At other times, Pansy would tell people she was a new employee. While working with Crystal, she was, almost always, assumed to be one of the many purchasing agents touring the company gathering ideas for a new perspective modeling campaign.   By looking, feeling and acting Prada in every respect, Pansy was reborn with a style all of her own.   No sooner was she back behind the private doors of the office she shared with Crystal, she would come apart with sheer excitement and renewed exaltation.   Her inner self was clearly the same girl she was before.

As the office door came to a close, Pansy fell against it with respiring breath and a glazed look of fantasy in her eyes.   "Did you see the way that guy looked at me?"

"Yes, I did."   Crystal boasted, admiring the

results of her own handy work.

"He was undressing me with his eyes.   If only we had a dance pole, I could have given him something to really gawk at.   Oh, and did you see what he did with that pole of his own…practically rubbing it against me?   Is this how it is with you?"   Still trying to catch her breath, Pansy tugged at the sweetheart line of her dress hoping to share more cleavage with her colleagues.

"I would cut it off if they dared to come that close."

"Huh…the S and M type.   I've heard about girls like you.   All business and stiff-collared on the outside, but low and behold, on the inside, fireball and whiskey with a chaser of whips, chains and candle wax.   Yeah, I've seen the type.   Well, don't you fret, sister.   I'm a quick study.   I should be up to your standards soon enough, ready to do battle of bondage with the best of them."

Crystal returned to her desk.   Hoping to get some work done and shaking her head in complete amazement, she uttered under her breath, "I think I have created a monster."

From behind the threshold of Pansy's office, a voice spouted, "A sex monster. You created a horny sex monster.   You left out the best part, sister."

"We have a meeting in one hour.   Would it be too much to ask of you to get me the file on the Max Factor account for the Fallbrook clients?"

"I need a bigger mirror in here.   I can't even see my shoes.

"Pansy?"

"Yes, boss.   Already ahead of you.   On your window desk, look to you right, next to your inbox and under the last month's issue of Vogue."

"What would I do without you?"

"You could start by getting me a bigger

mirror.   Then you wouldn't have to *do* without me
."

     For the next two weeks Pansy spread her
wings, *so to speak*, getting to know her inner self as
she also got to know a few of the guys she had her
eye on.   Though she kept her professionalism at the
proper standard at work, she did as anyone in her
Ferragammo shoes would do, and partied with the
rest of them.   Or the *best* of them, as she would say.
     The work place would never be the same.
What was once a man's business has soon
transformed to a business with a woman's
perspective.   Sales continued to increase as Crystal
controlled the reigns guiding the company into a new
era.   The older board members, who disagreed with
change, were soon relieved of their positions.   And
those who might have been left with doubt in their
minds quit of their own accord.   It was her baby
now.   Daddy had given birth to a multimillion dollar
business.   But Crystal nurtured it, perfected it,
smoothing out the rough edges, and feminizing the
personality of sales and product.   Marketing would
never be the same.   The era of the computer was the
next generation to take hold in her daddy's archaic
system.   None of the old guys would ever have
imagined what was about to occur worldwide, much
less under their own noses.   The mid eighty's were
the dawn of the computer generation.   Anyone with
a dream or even a clue could see the possibilities in
such an advanced technology.   Bradley, DJ, and
especially Billy had the vision well in hand.   Those
who didn't take advantage of the change in time
would surely be in for a shocking surprise.   I think
we, as the baby boomers, were the lucky ones.   We
seemed to be more prepared for the inevitable
changes that would soon take over the planet.   It

was, somehow, bred into our blood to perceive the times.   We were the future and we knew it.   And as history would unfold, we were right.   Soon after the newest computer system had been integrated into Worthington Products Inc. Crystal, Bradley and DJ had managed to coin a new phrase proudly referred to as *gamafication*.   It's meaning ties the gap between business and customers.   Or, better refined as product to client relationship involving free samples and better access to visual aids.

With everyday becoming a new dawn at Worthington Products Inc., Crystal was respected as the new business mogul to have successfully conquered the world and monopolize the products of feminine appetite for beauty.   The mere name, Worthington Products Inc. and beauty became systematically synonymous in every conversation. With the marriage of business to computers, both DJ and Bradley also become very useful to her trade. Working on commission, the boys were able to act as contractors in setting up the new system in Crystal's building.   In every sense of the word, the symbiotic relationship between Crystal and the boys was profitable as it was a step forward in the status of their posterity.

Crystal and Pansy soon became what appeared to be a pair to be reckoned with.   Pansy was Crystal's right hand.   Messages intended for Crystal's eyes and ears were just as certain to reach her, passed through from Pansy.   Climbing up the ranks of status, Pansy worked well with the changes in the company.   She was reliable and efficient as Mr. Worthington had, no doubt, discovered her to be. The man certainly had an eye for talent and potential. Finding Pansy was just one of many fortunate finds accredited to Mr. Worthington.   Of course, no one will ever know if the man ever saw the quirky side of the girl.

As business went on, Crystal's attention would be needed in nearly every facet of the company.   Bob was her head CEO in sales.   It was his expertise that kept all the clients satisfied with the product.   The more Crystal worked with new lines of product ideas, the more she would have to become involved with Bob's duties.   Much like her father, Crystal always kept business on a professional level. Never deviating in any way, she was the same machine her colleagues expected her to be.   Though time and time, again Bob would make his approach as subtle as possible, she shut him down at every turn, with Pansy drooling close by.   With Pansy at her side throughout the day nothing could ever be misconstrued as a casual rendezvous.   All meetings and brushes in the hall were as robotic as she intended.   However, one particular day seemed to turn all known tradition on its head in less than two point two seconds.

Bob was on the phone seemingly very distraught over a domestic issue.   "Honey, I'm sorry there is nothing I can do about it at the moment.   I have to work late tonight to ready myself for a very important presentation early tomorrow.   You know how chaotic it gets for me at the beginning of the week.   Well, you know I have already reserved the weekend for us.   Hopefully, then we can get together, make some phone calls and figure out how to deal with this unexpected pregnancy.   The last thing this world needs is another barking mouth to add to the population explosion."   Bob was not a believer in using the speakerphone.   It was his sworn duty to keep business private as well as his private life, his business.   However, the one sided conversation was very incriminating in Crystal's eyes.   "Yes, of course, I'm disappointed.   And I will do everything in my power to take care of this mess.   But there isn't anything I can do about it now, honey.   Yes, I will see you when I pick you up.   I love you, too."

Crystal stood at the door motionless and silent.   Both she and Pansy heard the entire conversation.   It wasn't her intention to be eavesdropping but the door was ajar and she couldn't seem to help herself.   Once she gained her composure and took in a deep breath she knocked at the door.

Bob responded as always with a big sexy smile and a savvy personality.   "Well, hello girls. Come on in.   I was hoping to hear from you concerning the Faberge account."   With little regard to the conversation he had just concluded with his girlfriend, he seemed to keep the same come-on look on his face along with the brass of confidence used to woo Crystal at every opportunity.   In her eyes, however, he was just a dog in dire need of neutering like all the others.   "I had some ideas to discuss with you, if you have moment."

Crystal placed two of the files that she had brought with her on Bob's desk.   Her stoic expression remained no different from usual.   But the words that came from her mouth proved to be anything but.   "I can only thank God I never once took you seriously, Bob.   Of all the lowest of lows. You must really think you're really something, too. I think that's the part of your hypocrisy that keeps me a single girl.   The prig sitting so high and mighty among his soccer trophies and sponsorship plaques." Crystal never before took the time to examine Bob's office before, but thought she would see examples of his womanizing ways.   "If only these people knew just who you really were."

Bob sat back smugly in his chair waiting for her to finish.

"I'm sure any one of the other corporate heads would be happy to hear of your ideas.   I, for one, have had my fill of your ideas and proposals." Crystal turned to the door nearly knocking Pansy over.   "I need to get out of this office, Pansy.   The idea of spending another second with this misogynistic bastard just makes me sick to my stomach."   The two exited Bob's office without another word.

Just short of rounding the corner of the first corridor Crystal seemed to have momentarily lost it, mumbling and growling obscenities under her breath.

"Did I miss the memo?"   Pansy said, scratching her head.

"What memo are you referring to, Pansy?" Crystal said, still in hate mode with a pragmatic and robotic vernacular.

"Ouch.   Hey, girl this is me, remember?" Pansy further mocked her friend attempting to sound equally robotic, impersonal and brass.   "What memo are you referring to, Pansy?   The one that says to pick out the most gorgeous hunk in the building and totally bash him.   That memo, Ms. Worthington." Pansy mocked using her bass voice and scrunched up facial expression.

"I don't know what my father was thinking when he hired that bastard."   Crystal barked.

"Okay, girl this is me waving the white flag. You can put away the voodoo pins now."   Pansy waved her hand in Crystal's face trying to get her attention.   "What are we talking about here?   Bob is your best sales rep this company has ever had."

Just short of making it back to Crystal's office, the tears were pounded back by her anger.

"Yeah, a fucking salesman to the end."   Crystal barked, slamming the door behind her.   "I'm glad *I* didn't buy into any of his bullshit."

"Something tells me you did more than make a purchase, sweetie" Pansy looked closely into Crystals stewing brown eyes.   Not only was Pansy clever around the office and office machines, the girl could read her friend just as easily as reading the first line of an eye chart from three feet away.   "Are you two…?   Oh, damn, you are."   Pansy's look of inquisitiveness was all reading.   "For how long?"

A single tear gathered at the corner of one eye before tracing a path down her cheek. A familiar knot at the top of her stomach took it's time pressing a painful pathway to the pit of her gut.

Reading the answer on Crystal's expressionless face, Pansy cooed,   "Oh, girlfriend, I am so sorry."   Pansy tried to console to no avail. "I had no idea, sweetie."

"And no one will."   Crystal cried out, unable to hide her emotions any longer.

"My lips are sealed.   I swear on my Movado watch."   Said Pansy, holding up the Boy Scout three fingers.

"That son of a bitch.   He is so fucking smug, thinking I wouldn't figure him out.   I could just scratch his eyes out and feed them to his slutty girlfriend."

"How far did you two…?"   No sooner Pansy spoke the words, she read the answer.

"Well, at least we know he's not a Eunuch."

"Pansy."   Crystal snapped, showing little appreciation for her friend's attempt at levity.   "The only difference between Bob and the other reps is they *know* they are ass holes."

"That's right sister, we need to go out, get drunk and buy me more shoes.   Or get the shoes

first, which ever you prefer.   I'm okay with either.
Just don't get too drunk to sign your name on the
tab."   Pansy would babble on.   It was her attempt
at comforting.

"Pansy, you're not helping.   I'm trying to be
pissed off here." Half heartedly, she tried to remain
mad.

"Exactly!"   exclaimed Pansy. "What a
serious waste of time.   We should skip pissed and
go straight to drunk.   Or there's always my best
friend, Mr. Rocky road, or Mrs. vanilla with hot
fudge."   She said with fluttering, dreamy eyes.

"That does sound kind of good."   Crystal
moaned through her sobering tears and a red face.
"But I think I still need to hit something."

"And…there's always that."

"I have been so stupid.   He's such an ass.
Why would I think there was a man worthy enough?"

"Sorry, girlfriend.   I don't know if I'm the one to
ask for advice in that department.   My improprieties
sort of speak for themselves.   Although, if it's any
consolation, he was the best ass to have given into."
Pansy scratched her head in dizzying thought.
"Wow, I just had a deja va."

"Oh, Pansy, you really need to stop talking
about his ass.   I would much rather talk about
strangling him or at least brow beating him to death
for the rest of his years working here.   Or perhaps, I
should have him kidnapped so I could deal with him
on my own terms."

"Said with a bucket of enthusiasm dripping
with bitter rancor and some sadistic tendencies."
Pansy's mind wasn't ready to relent.   "I suppose it
would be too fresh a wound to ask how it was?"

"You really do need help."

"So I've heard.   But no complaints from any
bedfellows."

“Sit on a happy face and fuck you very much.”   Crystal retorted.

“Ahhh, there’s my girl.   Now let’s leave this joint and get some ice cream.”

CHAPTER 11
Crystal’s awakening

“I think the silent treatment and unanswered calls have gone on long enough.”   Bob said, making his way into Crystal’s office.

“Whatever do you mean, Bob?”   The way she pronounced his name would make a chalkboard cringe.

“I haven’t been able to get any of my work done.   I can’t eat.   I can’t think.   For three days now I have been putting the keys in the wrong door. I have--”

“Sounds like a personal problem, Bob. Perhaps you should seek professional help from somebody who’s *give a shit* isn’t broken.”

“That’s just what I’m talking about.   I don’t know what happened between us.   You at least owe me an explanation.   Nothing could be more unfair than to mislead me with such passion, and the next day, discard me like yesterday’s trash.”

“You know what they say, Bob?   You are what you feel.”

An odd sound came from the back office, momentarily catching Bob’s attention.

“It’s no secret how you feel.   I would just like to know why.   What did I do to deserve such topsy-turvy treatment?”

Pansy, who was in her office, was desperately trying to hear all she could by pressing her ear to the wall.

"Why should I tell you anything?   Do you really think I owe you something?   You got what you wanted.   Why are you here still here?"   Crystal was getting more belligerent by the second.

A sudden crash came from Pansy's office when she accidentally kicked a pencil sharpener off her desk as she was using her foot against the desk for better leverage.

"What was that?"   Bob inquired.

"Closet mice."   Crystal shouted, throwing a paper weight at the dividing wall.   "You should leave now, Bob.   I have work to do, and I'm sure you must have *somebody* to do."

Periodic sounds continued to come from the back room as Crystal kept throwing things in hope to detour her eavesdropper.

"I think I'm beginning to get the picture here."

"You think?   I didn't know guys had the ability to think.   I thought the other head did all the thinking."

"Oh…"   Pansy squealed aloud, feverishly trying to cover her mouth.

"What is that?"   Bob looked to the wall that had a paperweight still stuck halfway in the drywall. "Listen to me a moment, please.   I don't know what you are thinking or what you think you think, but I'm betting you got some wrong information.   Can we just start over and figure out how to fix this thing.   I really miss you, and I--"

"Want some more?   Do you?   I bet you do. No doubt, the best lay you ever had.   Quite the conquest I'd say.   Was it on a bet, or did you decide to do me all on your own?   Is that noise we hear behind the wall your buddies on the other side giggling and laughing, betting I would fall for your plea?   Fuck you very much, but, no thank you just the same."

Another item fell off Pansy's desk as Crystal threw a handful of pencils at the wall, dislodging and knocking the paperweight to the floor with a thud.

"Go on now, tell your buddies you lost the bet, or won, I don't give a shit which."

"No…I'm not leaving."   Bob remained, standing his ground.   "You owe me an explanation. We had a passion that was beyond words, and I know you felt it too.   There is no denying it."   Though Bob was raised in America, his Italian accent would become more prominent as he would become more upset.   The very thing that, unfortunately, would excite Crystal to no end.

"I don't know what you're talking about." Crystal was showing slight signs of running out of steam.

"Really?"   Bob said, stepping closer to Crystal.   "You make that kind of love to all the guys."   His voice was more seductive than she had ever heard in the workplace.   "Two, three times a night?"

Crystal's mouth became dry as she swallowed deeply.   "All the time, with different guys every night.   Did you think you were something special?   Poor baby."

"Mannaggia!   (Dammit!)   Why do you talk this way?   We both know it's not you."   Bob remained adamant knowing what a mistake it would be if he walked out of her office.

"You don't know me."   Crystal somberly moaned.

"Better than you know yourself, Bella." Bob leaned close to face her.   "I know you will *never* find another, much less will you ever look for another if you continue to act the fool you are being now." His cologne, unique to his body chemistry, filled her soul. "I can see in those beautiful brown eyes a girl who is lost and misinformed. It would really be a shame to discount all that we have been to each other."

Though her steam was close to empty, Crystal resisted as best she could. "Tell it to somebody who cares, Bob. Like your girlfriend. I Don't--"

"Want to listen to reason? That's right, Crystal, you're not the only one who can finish other peoples sentences and thoughts. And let me tell you something, Crystal," He said, showing far more compassion with her name than she had with his. "If I had a girlfriend whose name was not Crystal, I certainly would not be keeping a candle of passion burning for *you*."

Sounding less certain, Crystal showed signs of beginning to doubt herself. "I heard you talking to her. I caught you."

"Talking to who?"

"On the phone. The other day. You got her pregnant for crissakes." Any other time Crystal would not have given the guy the right time of day. But on this day, she had a notion, she just might have made a crucial mistake.

"Pregnant?" Bob showed no signs of deception. He was either the best liar she had ever been up against, or he was genuine. "I got no one pregnant, Bella. At least, not for the last nine years."

"Nine years?" Crystal was slowly realizing what a fool she's been. Her voice became softer and filled with doubt.

"I have a young daughter. She's nine. Her name is Gianna. She stays with me on weekends, and with her mother on the weekdays. I was going to tell you about her before…"

"Does she have a pet?"   Crystal asked remorsefully with her broken voice trailing off.

Suddenly, Bob put it together as well.   "Yes, she does.   As a matter of fact.   Her mother would not allow her a pet of her own, so together, we picked out a golden retriever from the pound to stay at my house.   The dog in question was said to have been spayed, but around the time *you* suddenly forgot my name and number, Gianna found out her dog was pregnant."

Crystal placed her hand over her mouth offering nothing to say.   Her eyes would say it all. "She plays soccer?" said Crystal, with a squint and a guilty look enough to grow a tail to put between her legs.

"Soccer and baseball, but you must already know all that since you listen to other people's private calls.   So, do you eavesdrop on other people's conversations often?"

"I didn't know."   Crystal could not have been more humble.   "I'm so sorry.   I am such a fool."   Crystal's voice was a near whisper as her eyes were as big as melons.

"See the trouble you get into sticking your nose where it doesn't belong?   But, It's okay, Bella."   He said, placing his hand beneath her chin. "If I didn't know any better, I would think you were jealous.   And any Italian could tell you, jealousy is the root to fine passion and a good healthy soul.

"How could you possibly forgive me like that?   I treated you so horribly."

Bob smiled in response.   "I think you just proved to me all that I needed to know about you."

"You are amazing."   Crystal's eyes showed every bit of remorse they could possibly convey.

Just then Pansy's chair slipped out from beneath her.   She had been bridging her entire body across her desk to the wall trying to listen in.   What she didn't realize was the desk was slowly moving away from the wall under all the stress.   With the caster wheels still spinning and turning with a loud clatter, the chair hit the floor.   The reverberating crash was undeniable.   Unless a mouse weighed approximately one-hundred thirty-five pounds, and was close to six feet tall, there would be no way to make such a loud tempestuous noise from within the closet.

Immediately, Bob reacted, moving swiftly towards what he thought was the closet.   Upon first inspection it became quite obvious what he was seeing.

With a listening glass still in hand, Pansy was knee deep and entangled in her chair and sporting a very guilty look on her face.

CHAPTER   12
A week before the moment of truth.   Part 2

The club was packed with the usual crowd of hard working people looking for a fun place to forget about the work week and those who simply wanted to have a good time and dance.   The band was rocking the house down.   The aroma of steaks on the grill was coming from the kitchen.   The stage lights were putting on a fantastic display.   And the register was ringing it's tone with every liquor sale.   Life was good and I wouldn't have it any other way.

As Crystal searched the club for the mystery guest, we all seemed to harbor some curiosity as to who he might be.

"So, why did you two name this place "The Shot of Gold?"   Taylor slipped right back into her repertoire of long winded questioning.   "Seems like an odd name for a nightclub.   I mean…I would have expected a mining town to be nearby or shot glasses of tequila…"

Miranda seemed to be the one most obliged to answer.   "It's a long story, but it all started long before there were mining towns."   With a smile and the anticipated reiteration of her favorite story, Miranda began to describe every detail.   She loved to tell people about the time capsule and of our eternal connection together.   I have to admit, I thoroughly loved to watch her tell the story.   It never grew old.   Each time, she would mention some new facts that I hadn't yet known about.   And inasmuch as Bob and DJ hadn't yet heard the story either, it seemed most appropriate to go into full detail, explaining how life can be so amazingly connected.   My wife was best at narrating the story, giving expression and enthusiasm to every turn of event.   She had everyone's full attention.

From the very beginning, Taylor was enthralled by the possibilities and ramifications of every life and all the surrounding involvements. Every action constitutes a reaction.   It didn't take too long before she had everyone in love with Rosemary.   And when Miranda got to the parts of the story that involved the insurance company and how Rosemary went from a sophisticated corporate head to a silly, half-witted janitor, Destiny would briefly take over the narration to describe the silly quirkiness only she knew about.   Destiny had us laughing loud and hardy.   She certainly had a way of pulling the humor out of us all.   With a falsetto voice, Destiny would cry out, "Nuts?" and all of us would giggle and imagine the fun that old bird must have had being able to play such a role of anonymity and still be the one who owned and, for the most part, ran a huge company all by herself.   And when they talked about the part where Crystal knocked Bobbie out with the manuscript, all three girls clamored to be the one to tell Bob and DJ just how satisfying it was to watch such a monumental event.   Bob didn't seem the least bit surprised.   And of course, there was the expert performance by Crystal done on behalf of the local sheriff of El Mirage.   Bob seemed to enjoy the part about the impromptu role of the proper southern girl, accent and all, explaining her side of the story to the sheriff just minutes after she had walloped Bobbie into a submission of slumber.

We took a moment to briefly talk about Rosemary.   Instead of it being a somber discussion, we kept it uplifting by reflecting on each of our own stories of fun and excitement when working with her. My own input justified the very brilliance of her ways; instead of being a boss that would, normally require everyone would be on their best behavior, she hid her position from everyone allowing a natural and relaxed work environment.   Which, also, allowed her to get to know and see everyone as they truly were.   How cool is that?   We all agreed that Rosemary was many things to us all.   Those of us lucky enough to have spent as much time with her as Miranda and I knew her to be the image of true love and altruism.

By story's end, Miranda culminated by answering the all important question; why was the club named The Shot of Gold?   Quite simply put, had it not been for the *shot of gold* found in the time capsule, the club might never have existed.

Taylor looked to be astounded, and for the most part so did DJ.

Bob didn't seem the type that would overtly dispute his disbeliefs.   He took the story in stride, congratulating us with our success.   We certainly wouldn't expect everyone to believe our story, but Bob was reserved with his opinions.   Perhaps out of respect or maybe it was his upbringing that detoured him from showing too much of what was on his mind.   I had to admit, the more I knew him, the more I respected him and would, each time, look forward to his company.   Each meeting urged me to get to know him better.   If not so much for my own curiosities, but for the good of Crystal.   My greatest concern was for Crystal.   I wanted what was best for her.   Not to mention, we all made a promise to Rosemary we would reserve and assure the sanctity of just that.   If Bob was Mr. Right, we knew we would need to work fast to find out exactly who this was.   Because from my vantage point, I could clearly see the change in Crystal.   Whether we owe that change to him, that remained to be seen.

When Crystal returned she was in the company of a man with penetrating blue eyes.   She introduced him to us all saving Taylor for last. Immediately, Taylor jumped to her feet eager to shake his hand.   Apparently, she was the only one of us privy to his name and identity.   And true to Crystal's intuition, Taylor reacted exactly as she hoped and anticipated; with praise for the man and the highest show of respect and honor.

The blue-eyed man was impressed with her candidness and her obvious abilities.   No doubt, it didn't hurt matters that she just happened to

recognize his attributes to what seemed to be the
Rock and Roll world.   What was not so apparent to
us was, somehow, innately detected by Crystal.

His final question was rather an unusual one.
The blue-eyed man asked a few questions of
Taylor.   Each time, Taylor volleyed an arsenal of
answers.   Without a list to read from or even having
been primed by any forewarning, it was as though
Taylor knew exactly what this man would be asking
her.   He then showed her five pictures of prominent
people associated in the, behind the scenes, music
business.   I didn't recognize any of them.
Although, Taylor not only knew who they were but
practically new their entire biography.   In answer to
one question, she spouted off the top rated twenty-
five songs that were most frequently playing on the
radio.   She had me impressed, and I didn't even
know what kind of interview she was undergoing.
She was nearly answering his questions before he
was done asking.   And each time he would have to
stop her from going on.   She could probably have
named the one-hundred top hits in alphabetical order.

His final question was rather an unusual one.
Without hesitation he asked when she could start
working.

Taylor looked to DJ, and upon his quick and
unconditional approval she spouted, "Yesterday."

The man handed Taylor his card, asking her
to call him first thing Monday morning for her first
assignment.   "You have talent, young lady.   That's
what keeps my business running better than all the
others."   He thanked Crystal and managed to
quickly disappear into the crowd.

"Wow," Taylor shrieked, nearly shattering
DJ's eardrum, as soon as the blue eyed man was out
of sight.   "I got a job with Mr. Wenner.   Thank you
so much, Crystal.   I don't know how to thank you
enough.   This is a dream come true.   Oh, my God,

this is big.   Thank you, thank you so much."

"I had little to do with it Taylor.   You did it all on your own."   Crystal said, looking amazed as to how well Taylor had done.   "I don't think I have ever seen him so impressed.   Congratulations."

Taylor leapt from her chair, hopping and jumping toward Crystal. Taylor wrapped her arms around her like light brown haired Saran wrap.

We were all so excited and happy for her. Of course, not one of us was brave enough to ask who the fellow actually was.   Eventually, Taylor managed to settle back to her seat.   She looked to be on sensory overload as she kept thanking Crystal and hugging DJ.

"Ok, I'm probably the only one at this table who didn't recognize the guy, so would somebody please clue me in."   I looked around the table only to find the same curious reaction from everyone else. "Anyone?"   All but Crystal and Taylor shook their heads in answer.   "Who was he, Taylor?   Now, you got me dying to know, over here.   Who the heck is Jann Wenner?"

"He just happens to be the biggest name in Rock and Roll.   He rubs elbows with The Beatles, The Rolling Stones, oh heck, just name any band. He can make you or break you with just the mention of your name.   Oh my God, I cannot believe this day.   I have never been so excited."   Forgetting the question, Taylor went on with a little private moment of excitement once again.

Crystal simply folded her napkin while hosting a very smug grin of satisfaction or self-gratification.

"Taylor…?" I gave her a look, begging for her answer.

"Jann Wenner is the founder of Rolling Stone Magazine.   He is the God of Music journalism, politics and current events…" Taylor was just getting started. That girl had her facts and insight in perfect order. "Aside from the fact he doesn't believe in hand guns, the man is the soul of our country. He's--"

I could see she could have written a full thousand page biography on this man who none of us would even notice on the street. "Whoa, whoa. Slow down a bit, sweetheart." I knew the night wouldn't be long enough for this biographical recital. "I didn't recognize the guy, but we all know of him. But how did you come to know all this information he asked you?" I never would have known who those people were in the photos that he showed us.

"She's inquisitive," Crystal answered for her. "Just as Jann said, she has a talent. Taylor not only has an insatiable hunger for knowledge, but she somehow has an ability to retain information. I noticed it sometime ago. Perhaps like a birth-savant, she seems to come by her talent quite naturally. Some people, we know, store facts and trivia that are quite useless, boring and tedious." Crystal looked directly at Brad. "However, our young lady here has a penchant for the rich and famous. So now, she can do what she likes best, and get paid for it."

"What will he have me doing? What will my job be?"

"Just what you do naturally, kiddo. Probably anything from muckraking to interviewing the stars. The possibilities are endless. There isn't anyone he doesn't know. I'm sure you will be having the time of your life."

Making us all jump nearly out of our seats and skin, Taylor let out a screech that even the band had heard. "EEEk, can you just die, Baby? I'm going to rake muck and hobnob with the snobs."

She shook DJ's arm nearly pulling it out of his shoulder.

"Yes, baby.   I am so proud of you, and happy for you."

"For *us*, DJ.   This is for us."   Taylor noticed the slight change in DJ's demeanor. "What's up, Baby?"

"I'm just concerned that you'll no longer have time for me.   We just got a place together.   We were just getting used to the new schedule being as chaotic as it is with you spending so much time at the diner and me at school."

Taylor seemed to be confident with the situation. "No, Baby.   It's not like that.   It won't be like that.   This is a good thing.   But…I can understand your concern.   Let's try to see how things go.   If we agree that my new job is not the right move for the both of us, you can quit school and I will support the both of us."   Taylor's silly humor and sideways reasoning seemed to ease the tension.

"That's not quite what I had in mind, my little upstart."   DJ teased, feeling reassured that she truly understood his pertinent insecurities."

"I have a good feeling the two of you are going to work this out just fine."   Destiny gave her positive assurance, perhaps more from her gifted insights than pure conjecture.

"I hope you're right, Des.   As happy as I am for her landing this fantastic position, I just hope some handsome rock star doesn't try to sweep my girl away with him.   Who knows where Rolling Stone might have her commuting to, and for how long."   DJ looked longingly at his girl.   "I can only imagine how lonely it gets out there on the road, running from interview to interview, job to job and so on…"

"Never fear, my love.   Nobody could *sweep*

me away from your love.   Who would dare?"   The two kissed, seemingly, assuring a seal of approval between them.

In the corner of my eye, I caught Bradley privately handing his girl a bite sized chocolate bar. I couldn't help but wonder if that was how he would secretly guarantee her devotion to him.

CHAPTER 13
A week before the moment of truth.   Part 3

After each of us had congratulated Taylor on her new position, the cocktail waitress returned with our drinks.   Following right behind her was a familiar face of an old friend who, apparently, came to visit with us and give us the news.   It was my buddy, ex roommate and one-third business partner, Billy.   After I made introductions and the drinks were placed, I went through the genealogy of our relationship hoping to bring everyone up to speed with who's who.   Not only was Billy once in a band with Crystal, but he had quite a business past of his own.   He was a man of many talents.   And though he I don't believe he was psychic in any way, he had visions of a different kind.   He was the seer of business deals.   He had an undying dream of what computers could do for humanity.   The things we would talk about, would have us up 'till the early hours of the morning.   He was always the guy with energy to burn, especially if you cared to talk about business, world peace, Popular Mechanics and the latest in technology.   I could tell he had a lot to share with us that evening.   He couldn't hide the excitement from us that was so obvious in his gleaming eyes that had way of smiling without any effort.

Billy immediately came to my side giving me and Miranda a big hug. "You guys will never guess who I just bumped into not five minutes ago!" Billy wasn't the sociable type so I figured the list of possibilities must have been quite limited. So I took a shot at guessing.

"Hmmm, let me think. Who is in town today? Hmmm…Jimmy Carter? Oh, no, it couldn't be him, he's out of town building homes for the homeless. Ron and Nancy are out of town…promoting some Star Wars effort." The response of hissing and boos was much to be expected. It was, after all, a tough crowd. "Gee…if snickers were candy I'd be knee deep in chocolate."

"Don't give up your day job, partner." Billy teased. "What is it you do, again?" Billy was like a brother to me, always telling me, claiming I needed to get a real job. "Oh, that's right you're doing it. I wish I could get paid for sitting next to a beautiful lady."

"Aren't you the sweet man?" Miranda responded. "But please, don't keep us waiting, Mike is about to wet his pants. Who did you see, if not one of the presidents of this country?"

Unable to keep his secret any longer, Billy answered with an abundance of enthusiasm, "Jann Wenner. Can you believe it? He's here in the club right now."

"How is it, even Billy knew who the guy was?" It was a rhetorical question, just the same, I was surprised to see Billy so in touch with the world outside of his own research. Then it dawned on me; Jann Wenner's paper often printed political articles about how the world needed saving from itself.

"We dropped out of school together." Proudly, Billy remarked.

Miranda seemed shocked, "When did you drop out of school?   And, more importantly, *why* did you drop out of school?   Where was I when all this happened?"

"It was a while ago.   Harvard had nothing to offer the entrepreneurial man," Or as he would refer, 'corporate incubators'."

"Jann Wenner dropped out of Harvard?" Taylor seemed surprised.   "I'm going to be working for a college drop out?"

Billy looked at Taylor wondering what she might have been talking about.   "Like I said, not all business people need the hardcore guidance of the system.   Some of us are actually quite capable on our own.   And…I have the proof."

I knew Billy was heading to a climax somewhere.   "So tell us what's the good news.   I know you didn't come all the way down here just to tell us you dropped out of school with Jimmy Carter."

Billy pulled up a chair and sat beside me. He had his wallet in hand as he began to tell us a story.

"Remember all those predictions I made years ago?   I had bet that the computer era would take off with no limitations.   We used to talk about robots doing the dishes and televisions the size of wristwatches."

Taylor couldn't be the one to wait for the final outcome of the discussion. "You invented a robot to do dishes?"

"Not exactly--" Billy looked at Taylor, perhaps wondering if she were ill or something?

"That's too bad.   Because I really need one of those for Grandma Tilly."

"Okay…I'm sorry." Billy hesitated a moment. He must have decided that she was mentally challenged as he chose to ignore her ramblings. "I sort of created a program that one day may lead to such inventive ideas."

"Oh, *one day* won't do. She needs this robot thing by Monday so I can go to my new job without leaving Grandma Tilly with too much work."

Billy looked at Taylor, tipping his head looking quite similar to the RCA dog with the phonograph. He then, opened his wallet and pulled out a folded piece of paper. "You remember that job offer I got from IBM a couple of years ago?" Billy did mention it to me, but I didn't remember the results of that proposition.

Bradley looked to be chuckling under his breath. "You took a job for a company named IBM?"

"I did. I took on a few tasks for them. And I wrote a program for them that I alone will be able to expand on in the future…sort of making me indispensable, which, by the way, they have already contracted me to expand on this idea."

"IBM…?" Bradley couldn't get over the funny company name. "You would think that they could come up with a better name than that. Am I the only one who sees the humor in this?" Bradley was the king of anagrams. *I doubt any of us actually thought of it until he brought it up.*

I could see Destiny squeezing his leg hoping to get him to drop the subject.

"I mean, really…I pee too, but I don't need to announce it to the world. I…BM?"

Bradley had a point, and it was pretty funny, but the timing *was* a bit off.

Purely out of respect for Billy's excitement, we all tried to keep from chuckling aloud. I could only imagine what Billy must have been thinking, that certainly, my friends were a bunch of AA drop outs or recently escaped lunatics.

Destiny's eyes got wide with embarrassment.

And Taylor bit her lip, holding back any laughter.

"So what was the result of your task?   I know that look.   I am dying to know what you have created, this time."

Proudly, Billy opened the piece of paper for us all to see.   "I created an operating system for the company and this is the first check for my efforts."

A loud whistle came from DJ.   "Now that's what I'm talking about.   I knew the future was in computers."

Taylor looked to be in shock.   Even though it wasn't a robot.

The rest of us congratulated Billy with jubilant excitement.

"It that for real?"   Exclaimed, Taylor, straining her eyes to make sure she was reading it correctly.

"I believe so.   It *is* the amount we agreed on."   Billy displayed a check made out to him in the amount of fifty thousand dollars.   "And…this is just the beginning.   They have me looking into the next phase of the project.   I already projected my proposal to them and they have just recently asked me to move to Washington, all expenses paid, to help oversee the new phase at another company called Microsoft."

"That is so cool, brother.   I always knew you would be the one.   All those wild ideas you would always come up with were, obviously, not in vain."   I was so happy for him and proud.   I knew that if anyone could change the world, it would be Billy with his profound ideas.   "So is this the first step in, you alone, curing worldwide hunger?"   Billy had a serious need to help those who were less fortunate.   And he wasn't the kind to think small either.   Global proportions were his way of thinking.

"I hope so, Mike.   After I finish with this project I would like to grow a substantial amount of capital to actually make a difference for those in need."

"And I know you will.   How long do you suppose you'll be in Washington?"

Billy quickly calculated the estimated work load. "This one could take me a while, perhaps two or three years."

"You mean to tell us that we won't be seeing you for two or three years?"   I was not prepared or happy to hear that my best friend would be gone for so long.

"Brother, I have been flying back and forth for the past two years already.   Did you miss me?" I hadn't realized he had already invested so much time in this project.

"I'm always missing you."

"*We* are always missing you."   Miranda added.

"Has it been that long already?"   Marveling at the lost time.   "I can't believe how fast the time has gone."

"And I'll be back before you notice me missing.   This project will tie in perfectly with a lot of the work I have been doing on my own.   I was thinking of calling it Doors.   So if you see a company called Microsoft jabbering about their new operating system you'll know, that's my baby."

DJ nodded, "I think that's awesome, Billy. What kind of format are you talking about?"

Immediately, Billy put his business cap on and began to describe his ideas to all of us.   It truly seemed to be exciting to see an idea grow from the ground up, and be a part of the discussion with its birth-founder sitting right next to us.   As the two computer programmers discussed the mechanics of the system, Destiny added an idea of her own.

"Can I see that?"   Destiny reached for the check that Billy was so proudly boasting.   She read the amount and who it was made out to; Mr. William Gates, fifty thousand dollars.   As she held the paper in her grasp, she went to work immediately.   Like a guardian angel, checking to make sure the road ahead was clear for Billy to travel, she put her magic to use. The vibrations went into high gear the moment her fingers touched it.   "If you don't mind me making a slight suggestion or criticism about your Doors idea…"

Billy was never one to object to any bit of opinion or criticism.   That was, after all, how he made it this far.   "Not at all.   What do you have in mind?"

"Well, I see the name 'Doors' as an undefined restriction."   Destiny claimed, handing the check back to Billy.   "I understand how doors can be opened to new avenues and ramifications, however, as a novice in the field of computers and such, I actually see '*Windows*' as a more visual and visceral avenue befitting to the ramifications that you just described to us.   It's only my opinion, but I would be more inclined to buy a program that appeared to be see-through and endless with clear openings and avenues."   She did make a valid point.   Though, I already knew she had better insight than the average consumer, I might have agreed with her anyhow.

"How intuitive…"   Billy thought a moment rubbing his fingers against his chin as he would do when deep in thought.   "I think you're right, Destiny.   I will bring it up to the board and see what they think."

I don't know about the others, but I was very impressed with my little sister.   And not to mention, how excited I was for Billy.   I hoped that the two years wouldn't make him too scarce.   We truly did love his company.   DJ, Billy and Brad talked shop for several minutes.   DJ had some fantastic ideas of his own.   If I hadn't already seen a well defined future for these three already, I would have thought they might have made quite a profitable quorum on their own.   Before Billy announced that he had to catch a flight that evening, he took DJ's number and bid all of us a good night.

No sooner my buddy and partner was out of earshot, I showed my pride in him, "Not bad for a collage dropout.   Of course, his astounding IQ of 170 doesn't hurt much."

"170?   Wow, that's genius."   Announced Taylor.

"Yes, it is."   Added, Bradley.   "I believe anything above 160 is regarded as genius."

"And what's your IQ, Brainman?"   Crystal spouted.

"159."   Bradley answered, somewhat diminished.

"Oh, how sad."   She poured on the sorrow voice.   "That must really irk you, always coming up one short?"   Crystal's banter was primed and ready for a full night.

Bradley kept his temper in check as usual. "I'm a good eight inches taller than you, Crystal.   At least I'm not a pint sized midget."

"Good things come in small packages, Nerdman.   Oh, I know just how you must feel. This happens to me all the time…you don't know whether to hurt me or grab me and kiss me in a moment of torrid passion.   You--"

"No, Crystal.   I just want to hit you." Bradley interrupted, perfecting his better timing.

"Ooo.   Got some points for that one, cowboy."   Destiny proudly announced, planting a kiss on her boyfriend's cheek.

"Go ahead, enjoy your nerdvona for now. It won't last."   Crystal retorted, showing good sportsmanship in the tournament of insults.

"Sitting between you two is like being nag-witched, with only Miranda and me between."   I thought to change the subject.   "…speaking of S & M."

"Great segue, Babe."   Quipped Miranda.

Well, I thought so.   I turned my attention to DJ. "Have you had the time to discuss your ideas with Bradley?"   I knew that DJ had some fantastic ideas, but I believed that Bradley had an integral ingredient to make a side business work rather well together.

"Not exactly."   both boys answered, shaking their heads with curiosity.

"Well, let me be the catalyst that makes for a hot idea.   What you may not know is the fact that we have a prolific author among us.   And I'm not talking about myself."   I could see Bradley already turning three shades of red.   "Our very own Bradley has published not one but two very sexy books on the subject of erotica.   And it's my better judgment--" I suddenly got a sharp jab to my rib.   "Okay, Miranda's foresight--" I stood corrected.

"Thank you, Dear."

"You're welcome, Sweetheart."   I answered addressing the formalities.   "*Miranda's* gift has brought something very interesting to our attention. With you, DJ, working on your ideas with virtual reality on a computer program, *we* believe that you could get together with Bradley and somehow integrate his stories with your program ideas.   I even came up with a catchy business name.   You could call it, VISUAL; Virtual, Instant, Sexy, Uninhibited, Adult, Lust.”

Immediately, Miranda and I witnessed the cogwheels of progress turning in their minds.   The two boys in unison agreed that our business proposal could actually work.

“With all the fear of sexually transmitted diseases running rampant these days.   What crime would it be to simply use a credit card to call upon a date via your computer.   And different from the videos that are only two dimensional you guys would be way ahead of the porn market with a three dimensional experience for your clients.   So, for a mere ten percent of the business--” I got another sudden sharp jab to the rib.

“It’s just our idea for you two to use it as you wish if you decide to go forth with it.”   reasoned, Miranda.   “However, we wouldn’t even have mentioned it if we didn’t already know that there was a market willing to try it.   And, simply put, I believe it will happen someday soon, whether you two create it or somebody else.   But I would jump on it as soon as possible.”   Miranda was right.   Once an idea is out in the open, it grows viral in no time flat, especially in the computer world.

“Has anyone asked you two to do some business counseling?”   Bob asked, eager to hear the response.

We both laughed and responded rather quickly.   “Yes, and we only do so for our friends and family.   We still have a young girl to raise and we don’t want to make public figures of ourselves. Keeping a low profile keeps us out of sight and out of mind.   The last thing we need or want is too much publicity.”

“That makes perfect sense to me.”   Bob

wouldn't be the first to think of such a use for our talents.   "Too bad though.   Just seeing you guys in action this evening, I see how you two could benefit a lot of people."

"That, we could, but we won't."   Miranda made our position very straight forward.

"We still live like witches, Bob.   The world is not ready for us."   I felt the need to add my input. I could almost feel how he might add a proposition to us that we wouldn't want to hear, or have to turn him down.

"You are a very unique family.   I have read about such capabilities in people, but always remained leery of the claims.   I think after today, I will keep a more open mind.   I thank you all for that."

"No need in thanking me.   I'm not gifted." Taylor's high voice and overt personality was always so refreshing to me.   That girl held nothing back.

"No?   Who just got a job working for Rolling Stone magazine.   You have the gift of gab, Sweet pea.   And don't you forget it."   DJ was quick to boast her abilities.

"And let's not forget she has a phenomenal photographic memory."   Destiny was only too proud to add.

"Do you really?"   Bob revealed another show of amazement.   "Is that how you were   able to recall all that music information earlier?

"To some degree, I suppose.   But I do a lot of reading about music, the stars and things happening in the movie industry.   Basically, like anyone else, if I have an interest in it, I will most likely remember most of what I have read."   Taylor hadn't before talked about her skill to us.   I felt equally interested in her input.

"Not quite like anyone else," DJ critiqued.

"Not just anyone else will be able to recall the amount of information her brain can store."

"I would have to agree with DJ."   Bob felt inclined to inspire Taylor's skill.   "I have a great many interests with my business, but I doubt if I would be able to show the kind of efficiency you were able to call upon tonight.   I still rely on my reports, documentation and the paper trail to get me through each meeting."

Taylor immediately went into gab mode. "That maybe so only because that is the system that you are used to.   I wasn't born able to do what I do. It took me time to develop my ability.   It first started out as a game with my grandma.   She was very involved with sports and the statistics.   She had a wonderful way of making sports more interesting by telling me the players' batting average and other attributes.   Eventually, I would remember the information as she quoted it to me.   When she realized that I was able to retain the information, she continued to challenge me with my school work, documentaries, and special interests.   Just about anything she felt I should learn, Grandma Tilly had me commit it to memory.   Even working at the diner when I was twelve, I was able to learn the menu with just a glance."

"That really is quite an accomplishment, Taylor."   The look on Bob's face was easy to read as he thought to challenge her.   "Are you actually able to recall what is on the wine list?   If you don't mind."   Trying not to put her on the spot, he simply had a deep Interest in her abilities.   *As did I.*

"That's nothing.   The things I have seen her do is astounding, to say the least."   DJ said, showing a great pride in his girl.

As Bob attempted to hand Taylor the wine list, she informed him that she had already read it.

From start to bottom, including the name of the print company that made the menu, Taylor recited every word and price aloud verbatim.   She hadn't missed a thing.

"I bet she could even tell us the license plate numbers of every vehicle she saw on the way over here."   DJ certainly held his girl in high opinion and pride.

"That truly is very impressive, Taylor.   A skill like that has unlimited ramifications."

"Like good journalism for a certain magazine."   Crystal boasted her agent-like prowess.

"Here, here."   Destiny held up her wine glass.   "To Taylor and her new career.   Good luck, little sister, and may all your happy dreams and fondest wishes come true."

We all bade Taylor our best wishes.   And by the end of the day, I felt rather proud of our gifted family.   Bradley was very excited to start working with DJ and his new program ideas.   Second only to Playboy magazine, Taylor would soon be working for the most popular magazine ever.   My business partner just landed a sizable commission with Microsoft.   And I had just made a deal with my daughter earlier that morning over Captain Crunch (Before the berries).   I was so impressed with another of her stories, she had written for me, that I made her a pinky promise.   I told her that if she were to continue writing such profound work of short stories and interesting narratives until she reached the age of fifteen, I would see that her consolidation of work would be published under her name.   And, that book would one day come to fruition.   It came to be called, *Philosophy, the Obsession*, by Samantha Shane

While most were busy talking about Taylor

and her phenomenal abilities, Brad and Destiny were busy cuddling and kissing.   Destiny whispered quietly to Brad.   Her smile was sly hiding beneath a very thin veil of shyness, but her eyes told a different story.

Bradley got an idea, no doubt to steal away with his girl, for a moment of privacy.   "Are you thinking what I was thinking?"   The music from the band had suddenly stopped, making Bradley's proposition to his girl obvious and less private than he had hoped and anticipated.

Crystal couldn't pass up the opportunity to get another dig in Bradley's side by obtruding, "Oh, my God in Heaven, you too were thinking that you were a total geek unworthy of flesh and bone?"

CHAPTER 14
The envelope.

Destiny took time off from work to undergo another eye examination.   Bradley had taken advantage of the timing and opportunity.   I'm sure he figured that Destiny would never have allowed it. He had given this moment considerable thought.   *I could only imagine that the excitement and anticipation simply got the better of him.*   He opened the envelope full of curious pre-conceived notions.   What could Rosemary possibly have to tell

him that had to wait so long?   The seal gave way as he tugged at the envelope.   Inside, he found what I might have guessed; it was just like Rosemary to be one step ahead of each of us at every turn of the road. Bradley found three items inside.   The first item was another sealed envelope with a note printed in Rosemary's shaking handwriting.   The note read; "This time, Bradley, wait until the time I had asked." The second item was a piece of paper with a note on it as well.   It read; "Inasmuch as you could not wait as directed, I will offer one consolation to you.   I leave you with two of my predictions.   Keep this information in mind when dealing with your business ventures.   Number one, in the year 1992 the Chinese will rise in power.   However, the day the larger percentage of the Chinese population forsake Buddhism for Muslim is the day you should be concerned about more than just business matters. Number 2, the year 2020 comes a new world power. Be prepared."
The third item in the envelope was a bandage. Apparently, Rosemary knew that Bradley would get a paper cut when opening the envelope.

        Bradley notified me immediately after applying the bandage to his finger.   We discussed the ramifications of the message.   I had assured him that he had plenty of time to concern himself with world affairs.   I believe this was Rosemary's attempt at a subterfuge keeping him from opening the next sealed envelope.   However, the very singularity that got me thinking was the fact that Rosemary knew that Bradley would be calling me with this information.

CHAPTER 15
The beginning of the end

I was especially looking forward to our Family Circle meeting on this particular night.   We had a fantastic band in the wings called Dokken who had a huge play list of good rock and roll, most of which was their own music.   Scheduled for that evening, we had also commissioned a talented comedian named Jim Carrey who had an uncanny way of contorting his face to impersonate a good number of actors, including my favorite, Clint Eastwood.   By the way, it wasn't long after Jim performed on our stage, he was contracted to do his first movie.   *"Bully for him," as Rosemary would say.*

Crystal came alone into the VIP lounge to attend our weekly meeting.   I jumped to my feet and approached her like never before.   I greeted her with an embrace that was tighter and longer than usual. The dream I had the night before stayed with me the entire day.   I was emotional and in my own way, feeling vulnerable.   I felt I needed to reflect my feelings, or at least, show my support to somebody who played a very important role in my past life. Perhaps this was my way of finally showing her what I never realized before.   The epiphany struck me the moment I held her in my arms.   Rosemary was right.   Had I never met Miranda, I never would have been able to let her go.   Even to the depths of Hell, I would have followed her all the way down.

Though Crystal knew and understood my idiosyncrasies, she looked me dead in the eyes and spoke aloud and shamelessly, for all to hear, "I don't know how to love you…and not love you."   She said, most sincerely.

"I was about to say the same thing to you." I then tucked her head into my chest and held her for what might have been an hour, for all I knew.   Time didn't matter.   Words didn't seem to either.   My tears welled up as I fought them back as best I could.

"Wow, quite a private moment."   Wide-eyed and mouth agape, Taylor spouted, always being the first to observe and report…aloud.

"Theirs is a love that transcends time." Miranda said, softly and quietly so not to rush or interrupt the moment.

Of course, the moment might have lasted a bit longer had it not been for Destiny and Bradley's arrival into the VIP lounge as well.   And as usual, Bradley would make his grand entrance, this time, by tripping on the only step that existed on the second floor.

In a nanosecond, the special moment had abruptly ended with Crystal on high 'Nerd Alert'. "Not yet house trained, Dork?"   Snapped Crystal, as she gave me a wink.

Bradley ignored her by helping Destiny to her seat. "Sorry, for the interruption, folks.   I hope we didn't miss anything."

Taylor answered somewhat jubilantly.   She seemed to come alive even more than usual when at the club.   I think Taylor really had a deep desire to meet anyone who might be of fame.   "Nope, no movie stars yet."

"Where's DJ?   Isn't he coming tonight?" Destiny, said finding her seat next to Brad who seemed to be having trouble with his tie that somehow managed to accidentally dip into a glass of ice water as he sat in his seat.

"Unfortunately, he couldn't make it tonight. He had to take a final at school, but he sends his love."

"How about you, Crystal, where is Bob?" Destiny took notice how empty the Family Circle seemed without Bob and DJ being with us.

"That's the life of a traveling salesman. Never around when you need an escort." Crystal threw a disgusted look at Bradley as he attempted to dry his tie.   "Really Bradley, you just got here?   You certainly don't waste any time making a fool of yourself.   I don't understand why you put up with this walking disaster, sister." Crystal said, shaking her head, addressing Destiny. "He's such a dork.   It's a wonder he doesn't fall down an elevator shaft.   Oops, been there, done that."

Destiny placed her hand at the side of Bradley's chin and guided him to face her.   Always at his side to defuse the treachery that Crystal would cause, she placed a gentle kiss on his lips while whispering just loud enough for us all to hear, "Put up with and put out for, my adorkable lover."

"Ewww!   Way too much information, sister. You two really need to put a lid on that behavior before you get here.   You know they serve food here?"   Crystal barked as she found a seat next to

Taylor.

"What's the matter, Crystal?   Didn't get any last night?"   Bradley said, showing little regard for opening Pandora's box.

"While I leave you in wonder, just begging to know about my private love life I simply ask that you go French kiss a cheese grater, you pencil-necked, backwoods baboon."

"And end up with a sharp calloused tongue like yours?   No thanks, my love life is perfect as is."

Crystal reached for a menu with one hand as she flipped Bradley the bird with the other.   "Hey, Dork, how many fingers am I holding up?"

The band was at the stage, setting up and conducting sound checks.   The regular dinner crowd was beginning to shuffle in.

The waitress showed up just in time, asking for our order.   The girls almost always order the same antipasto.   Brad and I, settled on meat and potatoes.

As the waitress made her way down the stairs, Crystal insisted on hearing one of Samantha's new jokes of the week.

I obliged proudly.   "When is a cat not a cat? Give up?   When he's a little hoarse."

"Oh, that was cute."   Crystal's maternal fondness showed no end.   I never thought I would see the day.   I never realized she was capable.   At least, not until I saw the real Crystal in my dream.

"Here's one I thought of on the way here," Crystal had always been my favorite comedienne. Though her best acts would be her impersonations, her delivery of jokes held no bounds.   "A man stumbles into a bar and says whoa, deja vu."

A long pause followed the delivery of her joke as we waiting for the punch line.   We hadn't

immediately realized the punch line was the joke.
That's when we started to laugh, realizing it was
actually quite clever.

"Wait.   I don't get it."   Taylor said, already
feeling annoyed with herself.   "Where's the joke?"

"I see it going in two different directions."
Bradley offered to explain.   "Deja vu, meaning the
man stumbling into the bar is already drunk and
seeing double.   Or, he got so drunk earlier that day,
he was experiencing deja vu when he returned to the
bar."

"Oh," Taylor put it together.   "Okay," she
said, nodding her head and fluttering her brown eyes.

"It's okay, sweetie.   I won't fault you for not
laughing.   I seem to do better at impersonations."
Crystal set the menu aside and eagerly looked to
Taylor for some insight.   "So, don't keep me
waiting…how did it go at your first week of work as
a journalist?"

Taylor drew upon a deep breath denoting the
onset of a very long story.   "Amazingly and crazy.
I love the people and the speed of things."

"Speed of things?"   Miranda said.

"Yeah, it's like all these busy people at the
paper are strung out on caffeine and adrenalin."
Taylor snapped her finger repeatedly.   "Everything
is done and said quick, quick, quick.   Time is money
and money is news."

"Sounds like your kind of people."   Destiny
noted an upbeat pace to Taylor's, already, hyper
personality.

"They are.   As my kindred family, always
on the go, seeking new leads and new stories.   I feel
so at home with these people.   I'm only an assistant
so far, but I can see the potential.   Do you know I
haven't seen Jann since that day here at the club?
He must really be a very busy man.   I understand he

is working on a new project…something to do with a health magazine.   I hear he is a monster to work with."   Jumping from one topic to another, Taylor was all over the map with no compass.   No one dared interrupt.   She was on a roll that needed venting.   I guessed this must have been what she meant by the speed of things.   However, I would think the others that she works with might be better practiced in less babble and more actual journalism.   Either way, it was fun watching her excitement escalate with every new story she reported to us.   *She was a little kid in a candy store given free rein to gather all she could in a limited time.   And damn, if she wasn't making the best of it.*   I had a good feeling about her new endeavors.   I believed she would, one day, make a very good journalist.

As far as I could tell, Taylor hadn't taken her second breath yet.   It wasn't until the waitress showed up at tableside with an armful of plates that Taylor showed any sign of breathing.

As the waitress placed the bill at my side, one of her other bills had managed to fall from her apron. The paper took on a life of its own, sailing past me and onto the floor under the table.   Bradley was able to use the tip of his shoe to rake it closer to his reach. He handed it off to Destiny to hand back to the cocktail waitress.   It didn't take any of us very long to notice the effects that bill had on her.   It was as if she got a carpet shock from handling the bill.   As Destiny reached to give the bill back to the girl, she had trouble releasing it from her grip.   The vibration took effect immediately.   I could see her reading the vibration as I was sure Miranda was too.   It took only a few seconds for Destiny to predict the danger when she finally relinquished the bill back to the girl.

"I've seen that look before."   Taylor was accustomed to Destiny's many visions.   "Is it serious?   Do we need to put on a life jacket or something?"   Usually, Destiny would make light of the visions, never wanting to cause too much worry to her family.

"No, the plumbing in the building seems to be in order, however I'm not quite sure about the price of a steak dinner in this joint.   Really, Mike, twenty-three dollars for a steak dinner and a Big Mouth Mickey?"   Destiny was trying hard to skirt from the fact, she was quite shaken.

"Yea, well, somebody has to pay for all this wonderful entertainment."   I answered, hedging from the fact that I distinctly saw something bothering my little sister.

"We're all family here, Destiny.   What did you see?"   Miranda wasn't pulling any punches.   "I think all of us are sensing something as well."

"That's just it."   Destiny said, not quite sure of herself.   "It's a very dark negative energy, but I didn't see the source.   I couldn't seem to locate the focal point of the vision.   It was too foggy.   Like these darned glasses that I can't seem to see through."   Destiny removed the glasses, folded them and placed them in the case in her purse.   "I just got this pair yesterday.   I have an appointment with the ophthalmologist next week.   Hopefully, the doctor can tell me what's going on with my vision."

Destiny's vision had obviously gotten worse over the recent months.   I lost count how many times she had been examined and, subsequently, received a new pair of eye glasses, spectacles as Rosemary would say.   "Let us know what you find out, Des.   I'm sure they will be able to figure out what's going on."

"I don't doubt they will figure out what's wrong with my silly eyes.   My concern is for their ability to fix the problem."   She said with a mournful sigh.

I think Destiny was fully aware of what Miranda and I both felt to be imminent. I could not imagine what it would be like to slowly be losing my sight. To not be able to see what beauty this world had to offer would truly be an unfair card to be dealt so far along in the game. An ugly travesty hiding among the mysteries of life only to be revealed as a reminder of our mortality.

"And if they can't fix the problem," Miranda said, trying to soften the blow. "Are you prepared for what might be the downside?"

"Modern medicine can only go so far. I have been preparing for this since before I found out about Millie. I'm not letting go of hope, but I think Bradley and I are prepared for the downside."

"Downside?" Taylor snapped, insisting somebody explain. "Who is Millie…and where was I when she was introduced to this party?"

"Millie was my name in a past life. Remember me talking to you about that?"

Taylor was in work mode, digging up what somehow eluded her in past conversations with Destiny. "I remember you telling me every detail except the fact that there was some downside. Mind telling me about this downside about Millie?"

With a hesitation, Destiny had trouble answering. But it was for her to say. Taylor needed to hear it from Destiny and no one else. "Millie was…" Destiny paused again, momentarily. The rest of us knew once the words were spoken there would be no turning back. The materializing reality would be confirmed like an announcement over the PA system. "Millie was blind."

"And that means what to you?" Taylor wanted somebody to spell it out for her.

"As both Rose and Miranda have explained to me, many of us take on physical similarities and characteristics from one lifetime to another.   It's, many times, unavoidable."

"So this means the downside is you becoming blind like Millie?   Tell me I'm wrong, because this sounds a lot like what you are telling me.   Please, tell me I'm wrong, Des."

Destiny shook her head in answer.

"You're just going to accept that as gospel and not even challenge it?   Just give up without even a fight?   What kind of crap is this?   This sounds nothing like you, Des."   Taylor's anger was bleeding through like a crack in a dam ready to burst at any moment.

"Honey, I've *been* fighting.   All my life I have been fighting.   My first pair of glasses was fitted when I was four years old.   I wish I knew how to fight blindness, but so far, it's been a losing battle."

"I don't know how you could take this so well, Des.   Is this for real?   Have they given you any idea as to what is causing you trouble with your vision?"   We could feel the panic in Taylor's voice.

"They believe it might be something called Macular Degeneration.   But I won't know for sure until after next week's tests.   And yes, I believe this is very real.   I actually didn't want to say anything until I knew for sure, but one other doctor has already said the same."

"And if they find out it happens to be this Macular Degeneration thing, will they be able to do anything about it?"   Taylor was feeling every bit of emotion that someone might feel for themselves had they been handed such a dark diagnosis.

"There's no cure for it, Honey.   I wish there were."

"Oh, my God.   I can't believe this.   How long have you known about this?"

"I didn't realize how serious it was until a couple of months ago."

"What are we going to do?   You won't be able to work.   You won't be able to--"   A single tear gathered at the corner of one eye before tracing a path down her cheek.

"I will be fine, Taylor."   Destiny moved her seat next to Taylor, holding her hand, she continued. "I will be able to work.   We need to modify a few things, but with Bradley's help and all of you, things will work out fine.   They have to."

Taylor wrapped her arm around Destiny's neck, holding her tightly.   I can't imagine what you must be going through.   I am so, so sorry.   I wish there was something I could do."

"You do.   You have.   Just succeed and be happy.   That's all I ask."   Destiny had always been more than just a friend or big sister to Taylor.   She seemed to play a role as a mother to her as well. The nature of their relationship was admirable as well as inseparable.

I began to wonder if there would ever be a Family Circle that didn't involve crying and sorrow.

The waitress returned with more plates of food.

"Kathy, who ordered steak from your section?"   Miranda asked the waitress, letting curiosity get the best of her.

"Aside from your table with two orders, would be the older gentleman of the two guys sitting at table four.   Downstairs at table sixteen a young lady as well.   Will there be anything else?"   Kathy answered with little thought behind our interest. The nice thing about the crew working for me is the fact they know not to ask any questions.

"I don't think so.   I will let you know if anything comes up.   Thanks sweetie."   Miranda answered, deep in thought.   She knew as well as I did that something was amiss.   Witnessing Destiny and her vibration technique had only confirmed our ominous feeling gnawing at our guts.

Without making a big fuss over what might have been a false alarm or just a negative vibe from an angry customer, I decided to walk the club. Once I was finished with my meal, I had excused myself to check on things around the floor.   I checked out the old guy at table six asking them if their meal was up to par, if they needed anything. And I checked the gal at table six, much the same. Nothing seemed out of place or suspicious.   As a precaution, I spoke with security, reminding them to be on alert.   My suggestion would never fall disregarded.   Miranda's and my reputation for sniffing out trouble was always respected and appreciated.   When I returned to the table I motioned to Miranda nothing to report.

"Did you warn security anyhow?"   Miranda was also on high alert.

"Of course."   I assured her.   "There's an extra man at the door, and one extra on the floor just for tonight.   Just as you had asked."

Though Destiny was hard of seeing, she certainly had no problem overhearing my wife and I whispering about our security detail.

"Expecting problems?"   Destiny asked quietly so not to cause a panic with Taylor.

"Just a bad feeling." I said, handing Miranda's and my dirty plate to Bradley to be placed at the end of the table.

"Have any clue, what about?"

"Yes and no."   I said, questioning myself. "Crystal, does your private detective still insist that

Peter is behind bars?"

"That's affirmative."   She proudly announced.   "He's got a lot of friends in low places though."   Just then, Crystal reached into her purse for some paper and a scissor.   She made some cuts to the paper making a bold letter T.   After placing the scissors on the table, she then showed us the letter and had us inspect it.

"What's this, a magic trick?"   Taylor asked, still slow to come away from her sobering sympathy.

"Sort of.   Just not a trick, or magic.   More like a riddle to see if anyone can solve it.   I learned this one from an adorable little girl."

Both Miranda and I had a strong feeling where this was leading.   We both had recognized the gold plated scissors that Crystal had conveniently had in her purse.   I handed the paper T back to Crystal.   She then proceeded to make three cuts across the paper.   Then, she disassembled the paper, instructing one of us to figure out how to put the paper back into the original shape of the T.   Taylor was the first to try, failing miserably, she handed it off to Destiny, who didn't fare well with it either.

As Bradley attempted to work at the puzzle, Crystal instructed him to hand off the papers to Miranda.   "Sorry, dork.   Only People with I Q's of 160 and above are allowed to try."   I think we would have had to add up all of our I Q's to match Bradley's, *but I would like to believe that was Chrystal's way of telling him that he was too smart to play along and would solve the riddle prematurely.*

As Miranda and I worked the puzzle, we found that the cuts were strategically made to curtail us from seeing the obvious.   Miranda made the final placement, eventually, solving the puzzle.

After the accolades were offered, the subject of the scissors was brought up in a nonchalant manner.   Crystal announced to us that the pair had previously belonged to Rosemary.   "Rose might have forgotten that she had already given me a pair. I think she would have wanted you to have them, Destiny."   Crystal wasn't wasting any time handing them over the table.   "And don't insult anyone by not taking them.   They must be nearly sixty years old.   Make sure you put them in your purse so nobody gets any bright ideas."

As Destiny took the scissors, she instantly felt the presents of Rosemary.   A smile came to her full, pretty lips.   Once she touched them, there was no mistaking the previous owner.   They were, in fact, a pair of scissors from Rosemary's sewing kit. But it was obviously more than just a kind gesture of posterity to be handing them over to Destiny at that particular moment.   Crystal was up to something and it didn't become clear until I noticed her check her watch.   It wasn't the gold Rolex that she usually wore.   It was Rosemary's watch.

CHAPTER 16
The beginning of the end.   Part 2

With Rosemary's proverbial watch on
Crystal's wrist, there was no mistaking that there was
some ominous event to come.   It was for our own
good that she felt it important enough not to tell any
of us of any details.   Though she was doing as
instructed, I didn't like being left out of the loop.
But I held respect for Rosemary's reasons.   I was no
one to question such a wise old soul and seer.   My
having foreknowledge of a fearful situation could
cause me or someone else to do exactly the opposite
of a normal reflexive reaction.   The only other
reason Crystal might not have been able to offer me
any information on the impending dangers was the
fact that Rosemary could only offer a time and place
of a certain event to take place.   Anything outside
those parameters might not have been privy to her.

Destiny examined the scissors after her brief
reading of the psychometric properties.   And just as
Crystal intended, Destiny placed the scissors in her
purse.   No different than when somebody tells you
that they have a bad feeling, we could only hope for
the best, and proceed with our day with a bit more
caution.

"How do you propose to help Destiny with
her work?"   Crystal asked, trying not to sound too
cynical and, at the same time, take our minds from
the impending dangers.

"As far as typing and answering phones, Destiny can do that blindfolded.   However, we decided to get her an assistant to help her with reading and filing."   Bradley seemed quite confident in Destiny's abilities.

"And you're okay with this, Des?   That's all you would want?   Certainly, there must be something else we could do to help."

"Bradley and I have discussed this situation at length.   We figure if there is anything we haven't thought of so far, it may not be that important.   And if it is, we simply will cross that bridge when we get to it, *with a red tipped cane*."   Destiny's humor didn't sit well with Taylor.

"That's not funny, Des.   I'm worried about you."   Taylor was always extremely sincere and open about her feelings.   The sadness in her was affecting us all.

"Please, don't take it so hard.   I have had lots of time to think about what might be to come.   I can deal with it.   I have lived my entire life knowing this would happen.   I always knew it was not a matter of *if,* but *when*.   I feel quite fortunate that I have made it this far without losing my sight completely.   And I have Bradley to help me through the hard times.   Besides, a person would have to be blind not to see how much this man loves me."   Destiny, teased, groping at Bradley's face and head, messing his hair and pinching his nose in the attempt to mock a blind person.

Taylor wasn't able to show any appreciation for the humor as yet.   "I knew you were having eye troubles, I just didn't know it would be so serious.   I feel so bad now."

"She has all of us to care for her.   We won't let her down."   I felt it necessary to say what we were all thinking.

"There's also an upside to this actually." Destiny proudly announced.

"How could there be an upside?" Taylor challenged, the idea of blindness still tugging at her heartstrings.

"I solved a mystery today using my psychometric gift.   For some time we have been working on a particular case at the office."

Both Crystal and Taylor became very interested.   "Let me guess, the Walter Brooks case?" Crystal asked, very concerned with that case as well. In fact, everyone at the company felt something was amiss with the accidental death of the guy's wife.

"The very one.   We have all been very suspicious of the way this man's wife died, almost identical to the way his first wife died.   At first, we thought it might have been a very sad set of coincidences, but later, too many things were not adding up."   Destiny had us all wondering what this would have to do with her abilities.   "It wasn't until we got the autopsy report that also came back inconclusive that gave me an eerie feeling about this man.   The science of medical forensics can tell us only so much.   But in our business we have to work with what the doctor and police investigators say, however, that doesn't mean we can't do a little investigative work of our own."

"Did you go to the man's house and catch him with a new lover already?"   Taylor asked, denoting that's probably what she would have done.

"Even if I had, we would still be obligated to pay the hundred thousand dollar insurance policy to Mr. Brooks.   It's not illegal to have a girlfriend. And in many states it's not grounds for divorce to have an affair either.   But it is however, illegal to murder someone in order to collect on their policy. Double indemnity or not."

"No way!"   Crystal nearly pounced from her seat.   "Did you really?   You found some evidence against that S.O.B.?   Anything incriminating enough to put him away?"

"Put him away and then some.   As we speak, the District attorney's office is having his first wife exhumed for evidence of the same foul play."

"How on Earth did you accomplish this?" Crystal had to know.

"I wasn't able to get anything out of the paperwork that Mr. Brooks had filed before his wife's death.   So I interviewed the wife."

"You what?"   Both Crystal and Taylor spoke at once.

"The dead really can talk."   Destiny said, feeling quite proud of herself.   "Before you ask. No, Mrs. Brooks didn't come to me as a ghost or spirit.   Bradley and I paid her a visit at the morgue."

"Oh, that's just sick."   Taylor said.

"Maybe, but we must have made quite an impression on the pathologist down there.   We told him we suspected foul play and they gave us free range to investigate.   My eyes were so bad yesterday, I couldn't see if it was Mrs. Brooks or Mr. Brooks, himself lying in there.   So I held her hand in mine."

"Oh, my goodness.   You didn't.   How could you stand it?"   Taylor said with a squeamish look drooping from her face.

"I don't know, really.   I just felt like it was my duty to help this poor woman.   I just had a feeling I would be able to find out what happened to her.   It was like reading a book.   Once I held her hand I saw it all.   The power of psychometry was like never before, stronger, more vivid and all telling. It was as though she were talking to me.   I saw her getting sick at first.   It took weeks before she was finally taken to the hospital. And just like the reports I read in the office, the doctors at the Emergency Room had no idea what was happening to her. The ailments seemed too wide spread to pinpoint to any one disease. She was sent home seven times before she finally fell comatose and was taken by ambulance to the hospital where she finally died a week later. But that's not the kicker. She might have survived had it not been for the fact that her husband continued to poison her while she laid defenscless in that hospital bed."

"We suspected poisoning, but each of the attending doctors said there was no trace of poison." Crystal questioned.

"Yes, that's true, but they don't routinely check for arsenic. Aside from the obvious cost issues, it's simply not part of the common regimen for scrutinizing causes of deaths. The husband had been slipping her, low undetectable doses of arsenic for so many weeks, it simply went without notice. Aside from the darkening of her fingernails, there was no trace evidence of anything to go on. But here is the real kicker. All I had to do was tell the specialist at the morgue that I smelled arsenic. They checked with the lab and found that I was correct. I merely explained to them that my blindness had heightened an acute sense of smell. They never once questioned it. Immediately, after the lab found evidence of arsenic, the judge granted a search warrant for Mr. Brook's home where they found arsenic in his workshop."

"You did it, Des. You really did it." Crystal announced with amazement. And justified confirmation. "You broke the barrier that would have kept us guessing forever. Do you realize what this could do for the future of the company? Your gift will put those sons of bitches away before they know they've been caught.   That son of a bitch really killed her.   All this time we had a feeling…but you took it one step further, Des.   What ever made you think of going down to the morgue?"

"It was Bradley's idea.   He could see how we all seemed to feel the same eerie suspicions about the guy.   And how he was in such a hurry to get his wife cremated.   Without any real hard evidence, it seemed to be the only logical thing left to do.   And I don't doubt they will find the same results on his first wife, whose family refused to have her cremated." Destiny planted a tender kiss on Bradley's cheek. "So you *see*, please excuse the pun, it doesn't hurt to have a blind person help you to see clear to the path of the truth.   On the serious side, both Bradley and I have taken notice as to how strong my gift becomes with each day that my eyes grow worse.   It's like a magical trade off.   I seem to have been blessed with a gift that has yet to fully mature.   One only knows what opportunities will become available to us in the future.   If I continue on this path, I might be able to prevent crime even before people get hurt."

"Yeah, that will make people think twice about taking out life insurance on others."   Taylor boasted.   "Of course, I would hate to have to be the one to touch dead people.   How would someone get arsenic anyhow?   It's not like you find it at the grocery store under poisons for the family, chewable or easy to swallow capsules."

"It's hard to say."   Bradley responded.   "I doubt if the police will let us know where *he* got it. But it was once used in the gold and silver mining industry.   The arsenic was used along with mercury and other toxic elements.   It wouldn't be impossible to find, however, it would be harder to hide where one might have received it."

We all took a moment to sit back, taking in what Destiny told us.   It all seemed so wild and unbelievable.   Truly, Destiny could be the beginning of a trend in crime investigations.   Missing children, unidentified bodies and remains, could all become a thing of the past.   The ramifications were endless as well as overwhelmingly exciting.

Jim Carry did his fantastic skit on stage lasting thirty seven minutes.   The crowd was pleased, and still laughing long after he left the stage. The man had the ability to do the oddest things to his body.   From making his eyebrows wave like water, to dislocating his shoulder to fold behind his neck like a bird's broken wing, the guy was quite a contortionist.   I was especially pleased to see him do the Clint Eastwood impersonation.   I had a strong feeling that he had what it would take to make it in Hollywood.   It was a good feeling to see everyone in good spirits.   As the band slowly returned to the stage, plugging the guitars into the amplifiers and mikes back in as well, our waitress returned to refresh our drinks.   On comedy nights we encouraged our waiters and waitresses to tell jokes to the patrons.   It was just another way of helping the kids get good tips.   Kathy, our waitress, offered us her joke that was X rated.
        "You know how certain products and brands are named after the application they offer or represent?   For example; Tarn-X is self-explanatory. Band aids, and toothbrush also leave no ambiguities. Same goes for lubricant, it's simply been misspelled over the years.   Originally it was called and spelled, lube her c**t.   Don't shoot me if you don't like the joke."   Kathy spouted.   "I'm not the author.   I'm only the messenger.   Tonight is comedy night."
        Soon after the waitress took our order and

left, Crystal decided to offer another of her jokes to ponder.   "A less fortunate man living in New York was asked what he would do if he won the lottery. He simply replied he would be poor no more. Months later, the same man surprisingly won the lottery.   He was seen driving a modest car with a personalized plate reading, *po no mo*."

"Oh, I get that one."   Taylor was quick to announce her genius while offering a couple of chuckles.

Bradley then offered us a riddle of his own. "Say I hand you two American minted coins.   The two coins amount to a total of fifty-five cents. However, one of the coins is not a fifty-cent-piece. How can that be?"   Bradley said, seemingly quite confident with his riddle.

"*One* of the coins is not a fifty-cent-piece because it is a nickel."   Crystal was quite clever to quickly guess the answer.   "Where the other coin is a fifty-cent-piece."

"Not too bad, give the lady a goldfish." Bradley said, still sobering over her cleverness.

Immediately, Crystal had to boast a riddle of hers.   "A guy named Bradley, living in Los Angeles cannot be buried in his own hometown of Los Angeles as according to law.   How can that be?"

Bradley already knew the answer but chose not to say a word.

Taylor felt so inclined to ask for the answer. "Okay, I give up.   Why can't he be buried in his own hometown?"

"Because, unfortunately, anyone still *living* cannot be buried."

"Hey, ya have to admit, that was kinda funny."   Taylor laughed.   "I have to remember that one."

The jokes and riddles continued round and

round until the band started up for the final play list of the evening.   It was hard to believe that the night was already nearly over.   It seemed the Family Circle meetings went quickly.   Too quickly.

"Speaking of being buried," I had to ask Bradley an important question that was nagging at me all week.   "I had this really depressing dream about the black plague of Europe and I was wondering what significance this one strange message might possibly mean to you.   I figured if anyone might understand the history of the European plague, it might be you, brother."

"What was the message?"   Bradley was already intrigued by the historical value of the dream.

"Find Delta 32.   I know it sounds rather strange, but all through the dream I am reminded to find Delta 32.   I have no idea what it means."

Bradley many times before helped me with some of my dream interpretations from a historical point of view.   I figured that if Miranda couldn't help me find some answers, perhaps Bradley could. And as sure as rain, Bradley had the answers stored in his brain for me to simply ask.   "In the fifteen hundreds there was no study of genes or diseases, for that matter.   They had absolutely no medicines to fight a disease as the Black Plague.   No one living in the fifteen hundreds could have found Delta 32 because it wasn't discovered until four-hundred years later.   Delta 32 was discovered to be the gene that is immune to the black plague.   But only one in a hundred possessed that gene.   During a three-hundred year time period it was said that over seventeen million people died from the Black Plague."

"So this Delta 32 thing could not have been understood or discovered by anyone during that time period?"

"That would be correct.   It would have been impossible for the time."   Bradley said, hoping to help with more information.   "Do you suspect that this was another period in which you were living?"

"Yeah, I was some kind of a healer of sorts trying to help the public during this horrid time.   But the Delta 32 thing was constantly nagging at me to find it…or something."

"Rest assured, Michael, that would not have been possible at all.   I'm sure that if you were a healer, you did all that you could.   They had no microscopes powerful enough to understand the properties of such a small scale bacteria.   At that time, who would have thought such horrific devastation could have been caused by something so small as flea bites on rats and, sometimes, other rodents?   There was one particular healer that understood the connection between cleanliness and the possibility of contamination.   He alone was able to spread the word to keep the dwelling and body clean.   But nobody understood that the primary culprit of the wide spread of the disease was caused by the fact that the food source of nearly every household was contaminated with rat droppings."

I knew Bradley was reading more into what I was revealing.   Thankfully, he resisted asking any further detailed questions.   He understood that it wasn't like me to call attention to myself.   And having just recently found out that my name, in a past life, was Michel de Nostradamus, would no doubt, have been too much to reveal at a family Circle meeting.   Especially knowing that my wife of that time period was sitting at the same table as us.   I wondered how long it would take Bradley to put it together.   That is, if he hadn't already done so. That was, after all, the first time he had ever referred to me as Michael.

CHAPTER 17
The beginning of the end.   Part 3

Bradley was definitely a scholar of information.   His knowledge of semi-non-essential history helped me tremendously find the facts that I would be searching for.   Finding that I was once a prominent healer in a past life had me confused. The information that I learned from Bradley was monumental with my own self-discovery and research.   Nostradamus was an amazing man.   His abilities would hold attributes to the history books forever.   He wrote a number of books foretelling the future by way of the alignment of the stars.   He was the patriarch behind the perfecting of the Farmer's almanac.   His quatrains, to this day, still hold certain relevance in history books.   His prophesies held highest regard with the public as well as with the hierarchy including the wife of King Henry who commissioned him to chart her children and husband. It was Nostradamus who discovered the impending death of the King, who would, at the age of forty one, succumb to an impaling injury to the eye inflicted in competitive battle.   All his prophesies would become his attribute to today's astrology.   The man was nothing short of a prophet.   The more I learned of his genius, the more confused I would become. In all my previous lives, I was a healer, a man of wonder with unlimited powers in the occult.   Where did these powers go when I was born into this world? Why, this time around, did I have only a limited amount of incite to the future?   Time and again, Miranda would attempt to console my insecurities.

But my failures to read the future as I could in the
past would haunt me to no end.   Had it not been for
Miranda, I may never have found the time capsule.
And had it not been for Bradley on that fateful night,
I might have died in my own club leaving my wife a
widow and my child fatherless.

I awoke that morning feeling depleted and
drained by another of my night terrors.
"Why do you let it bother you so?"   Miranda
said, trying desperately to console my feelings of
inadequacy.   She was good with the rhetorical
questions, allotting me no time to respond.   "I see
several reasons why you might feel this way.   And
I'm not saying that you are not as powerful as the
past.   I believe you have the gift in a different form
of the past.   What I see is a wonderful man giving
himself to everyone before himself.   You do have an
energy with a very high spirit.   What you don't
realize is everyone feeds off of it.   Who's to say you
don't have the power.   How would you know? With
all the time and energy you put into our club and your
books how much more could anyone give?"
"But--"
Miranda placed her fingers on my lips.   "Let
me finish. I know the club is your passion.   We all
do, and it's fantastic.   I wouldn't change that for the
world.   What you do for others is no different than
that of Edgar Casey or Nostradamus.   You and you
alone have launched dozens of careers.   Your power
from the past has transformed into modern day
relevance.   What you do in the present is virtually
no different than what you did in the past.   Medicine
has evolved to the point where healers are no longer
needed as they were in the past.   I go to school to
practice medicine.   Things have changed.
Everything, eventually, changes and evolves.

What's needed in today's world is what you provide to us all.   You give us hope.   It's in your books and in your club.   Hope is what the world needs today. Hope is sorely needed because there is such a dearth of it today.   Those who come to the club, come to see you, and feed from your energy.   Those you touch with the energy of your soul have the ability to retain your energy and then feed it to others.   In essence, you are touching more souls with the power and energy of hope than ever before with all past lives combined.   Really babe, with such a powerful realm of energy at your fingertips, I am surprised you don't see how obvious the answers are.   How could you not see what is so overt to all others around you? Besides,"   Miranda had to make a point of telling me just how some things are meant to change.   "I know how squeamish you are around blood.   You may have been a healer in the past, but today you are the giver of hope to the many which is far more powerful than the healer of the few.   And who's to say hope doesn't heal?   In a sense, you are a healer, Mr. Shane, Jason, MS found in a bottle, Nostradamus or whoever else you might be or have been…you are the greatest healer of all time whether you realize it or not.   I know that long after you and I are gone from this lifetime, your books will live on just as all the others of your past.   Those you have touched will continue to touch others, and so on.   The times are different, Babe.   We are no longer living in the dark ages.   With technology making such huge advances each and every day, you have been able to spread your word of hope to a greater number than any comparison of the past.   Whether you realize it or not, you are networking with greater efficiency than the past could ever have offered.   It might be time for you to stop living in the past, Sweetie.   We need to start thinking about the future, *our future.*

So what if we can't see the imminent danger that lies ahead?   Then I guess we will live like everyone else on the planet, blissful and positive."

"Yeah, but it doesn't hurt to have a little insight now and again."   My demeanor was radically altered by her words of reason and loving support.

"And sometimes, that very insight is what gets us into trouble.   Just let it go, Mike.   We don't need to read and foresee everything."   She said, wrapping her tender loving arms around me as she nibbled at the nape of my neck.   "Sometimes it is best not to see what lies ahead.   We both know what dangers can occur should history be altered."

The chills instantly ran up my spine and made my entire body quiver.   "Ooooh, you know I can't handle that."

"That's why I do it, silly.   I just love to watch you do the shimmy."   she said, planting little kisses at the nape of my neck.

I quickly turned around, tackling her to the mattress, preventing her from causing anymore spine tingling shivers.   "So, how do you like it?"   I teased, wrapping her arms across her midsection as I laid against her with my body and nibbled at her soft neck.

"Doesn't bother me a bit.   I happen to love a little affection now and again."

"Oh, so I don't give you any affection, you say?"   I tickled her at every spot I knew would drive her crazy.   Her begging plea for me to relent went on without my reprieve for a good long time.   She giggled, laughed and finally shouted when her breath would allow for it.   I made her laugh so hard she wet the bed.   With one last kiss, I let her up.   "Tit for tat."

"But I didn't make you pee yourself."

"How do *you* know?"

"Oh, well, perhaps I should check." Miranda lurched towards my pajama bottoms making every attempt to pants me.

"Did mommy wet the bed again?" Samantha was still rubbing the sleep from her eyes as she sluggishly walked into our bedroom.

"Yeah.   Mommy needs Pampers."   I quickly tittered.   "I'm so sorry she so rudely woke you.   I can't imagine what could possibly provoke her to make such awful sounds so early in the morning."

"You were tickling her, Daddy."   She said, reprimanding me with her tone.   She wrapped her arms around my waist as the three of us hugged in a moment of silence.

The previous conversation had everything to do with a scenario that had yet to occur and had me very concerned.   Though Miranda had made some valid points about living without the worry and concern for what can't be helped or prevented, I still had those nagging visions to contend with.   *How would I react when the time was to come?*   As I combed my fingers through Miranda's hair, she looked up at me as she sat at the corner of the bed.   She looked so beautiful and inviting with her hair still messy and her pajamas still tweaked to one side.   It wouldn't have mattered if we had just survived a twister, I still found her attractive and sexy beyond words.

"Rain check?"   She whispered.

"You bet."

"Don't worry about tonight, Honey. Everything will happen as fate has planned."

"Hmm."   I responded, thinking that fate was, in fact, the very thing I was worried about.

"I never realized how devastating the Bubonic plague actually was." Taylor commented on the information Bradley had provided. "Seventeen million people died from the plague?"

Bradley was quick to reply, "Which, at the time, was one third the entire population of the European nation. Could you imagine living when one in three people of everyone you knew had died from a plague? That would be two people from this table alone. And--"

"We get it, Brainman." Crystal seemed to have been getting depressed by the topic of our discussion. "I think we need a dessert."

"Oh, thank goodness. I was afraid no one would ask." Miranda chimed in.

With a wave of a finger, I summoned our waitress to bring us the dessert menu.

Of course Taylor didn't need to look at the menu, already knowing everything our club had to offer. "If I am going to eat another thing, I will need to make some room. Cheesecake for me with extra strawberry." Taylor announced as she stretched her legs before heading to the restroom.

"That actually sounds pretty good." Crystal agreed, looking almost guilty for allowing the mere thought of indulgence and decadence to enter her mind.

"Are you sure you couldn't pick up on anything when you felt the ticket from the other table?" I felt the need to ask Destiny one last time.

"Honey, leave the poor girl alone. Everything is fine." Miranda squawked at me.

Destiny didn't seem to mind answering. Though her answer was vague, it gave me more reason to worry. "No, it's okay, Miranda. I couldn't tune in on what or who was behind the bad feeling, I can only say that it reminded me of the time that I thought Taylor was in danger when she went to Vegas with that guy.   Aside from that, I sense nothing."

"There you have it, Babe."   Miranda added, "*Nothing* to worry about.   Stop stressing."

As the girls were busy poring over the menu, I was unconsciously tapping my foot beneath the table, deep in thought and doing everything Miranda had instructed me not to do.   Perhaps it's in our nature as guys to worry about what might be.   *'What if'* can be a terrible feeling.   Especially, when you are plagued by a bad feeling that you can't seem to shake off.

"Babe…"   Miranda looked to me as if she were waiting for an answer that I somehow didn't hear.

"What?"

She placed her hand on my leg that seemed to be tapping at ninety miles an hour.   "You are shaking the entire upper floor, Baby.   Relax."

It seemed the more she told me to relax, the less control I had over my fears and anxiety.   I knew something was amiss, I just couldn't figure out what to do about it.   We had already taken extra security precautions that night, and all personnel was asked to be on alert.   Unfortunately, it wouldn't be enough. I was certain of it.

Dessert was ordered and seven minutes later, dessert was delivered to our table.   As the waitress placed the cheesecake at Taylor's setting, Bradley attempted to stand up.   He announced that he would check on Taylor to make sure she was okay.

"Sit, Bradley."   Crystal commanded, realizing she acted a little ruder than usual.   "I mean, what would you do?   Walk into the girl's restroom unannounced?   Perhaps Destiny would be best suited to check on things since she's a girl and you're just a geek hoping for a peek."

Crystal did make a valid point, but when she checked Rosemary's watch again, I knew all my suspicions to be correct.   Something was up, and only Crystal was holding the cards to this dangerous game of cat and mouse.

"Good point."   Destiny complied.   "Eat your dessert and I'll give you something interesting to peep at later."

"We're trying to eat here, Des.   Don't you get it?   I don't want to go there.   The whole visual thing between you and the geek is just nauseating."   Crystal brayed like a wounded cat.

"Okay, Crystal, spill it.   I know something is up.   You keep looking at that watch much like Rosemary would."   I have had enough of this esoteric game-play.

"Even if I could, Mike.   I wouldn't.   You know the drill."   Crystal was very direct and adamant about making sure we were in our place.   "Timing is everything.   So don't screw with fate."

"Terrific, you've been talking with Miranda."

"Of course, why wouldn't I?"

"Why is it, the girls are privy to all the secrets while us guys are left out in the cold to fend for ourselves.   It feels like a conspiracy."

"You said it, not me.   Frankly, I'm not one to brag, but guys only manage to screw things up anyhow.   Face it, Mikey, you need to *relax*."

"What is with everyone telling me to relax? I don't want to relax.   I can't relax."   I didn't realize that I was just one decibel short of yelling.   I stood up from the table to stretch my legs and pace. I don't know if it was out of habit or necessity to pace around when under stress, but this was one of those times of necessity.   Aside from the fact that my dreams and feeling were on high alert that week, I could see that Miranda's breathing wasn't quite the norm for her.   She wasn't telling me something which made the situation all the more intense.   Like a pot suddenly coming to boil, the all intensive scenario that I so dreadfully feared, had come to a head.   I didn't recognize the guy, at first.   There was no way of knowing.   His disguise was impeccable.   And yet, there really was no disguise.

CHAPTER 18
The beginning of the end.   Part 4

The older man in question stood up from his table just twenty feet away from us.   His being in the VIP lounge only meant that he had waited at least five weeks to get this reservation.   He waited five weeks to do his worst and make his move.   *How could anyone possibly harbor so much hate, to lie and wait, as he had?*   There I was, face to face with a man who wanted only one thing.   I had dozens of dreams where I stood in this very predicament, but never could I remember what I did or how I reacted thereafter.   Like all the times before, it was though I was reading a book with no ending.   And there I stood turning the pages of mystery as they would unfold anew.   It was daunting.   There was nowhere to run or dodge.   He held a gun at me, full arms length.   I was trapped, cornered and totally defenseless against anything he might choose to do to me.   It was like nothing I could have prepared for. I was suddenly in a situation that I could not resolve. It was obvious there would be no reasoning with this lunatic.   His assaulting words held no secrets.   His words wafted into a fog of serial deafness.   I couldn't believe how helpless I felt.   To charge him would only mean a shot, maybe two, to my chest before I could close the distance between us.   *How much strength would I have left, with a couple of holes in me?*   The gun was pointed dead center at my chest.   Only Clint Eastwood with an armor chest plate hidden under his poncho could have seen his way clear out of this one.   His features were well hidden beneath his disguise.   The long beard and mustache were scruffy and unkempt.   Resembling a homeless man, his clothes were tattered and dark with stains.   His face looked to have been tanned or filthy.   I could understand how he would be less scrutinized at the door.   He was dirty and undesirable, the very kind that we tend to ignore or look away from.   The man with the gun had obviously spent a lot of time planning this moment. As I faced him, I knew I had to act, but my legs seemed paralyzed, glued to the floor in a bad dream that had no clear ending.   The girls had their backs to him as Bradley was the only one to see exactly what was happening.   The crazy man made one last gesture as he placed both hands on his gun.   There would be no closing argument or plea for reasoning. The moment had arrived as plainly as if it were written on the walls.   The muzzle blast was all I could remember, the bright reddish flame and smoke that emitted from the barrel nearly blinded me as the sound was deafening and painful to the ears.   Even over the one-hundred decibel sounds of the band the shot from the gun held no comparison.   The screams from the crowd seemed to follow in an instant.   In my peripheral vision I could already see the wave of people heading for the exits.   Oddly, I thought, my life didn't pass before my eyes.   Nor did things seem to move in slow motion.   It simply seemed surreal.   I felt nothing, no pain or discomfort.   I simply stood paralyzed.   It wasn't until the second shot had fired that I realized the only thing not moving was me.   I was the only thing not moving as everything around me was in fast forward and had fallen into place round my feet.   In an instant, I came to realize how every dream I ever had was the result of this very moment.   It was exactly the same.

I didn't remember any outcomes because there were none.   I had obviously died in every war that I fought with my brother at my side.   I never survived to know what happened next.   I either panicked or froze just as I had done this last time.   Almost every dream I ever had suddenly flashed before my eyes. The ridiculous redundancy of what people would say about the death experience would come to be true after all.   But there I was, still standing, feeling nothing and hearing the last of the screams of those rushing to get out of the club safely.

Then, like something out of a movie where an unsuspecting hero arrives and saves the day, the scruffy old guy fell to his knees and then to his face, planted on the floor where he stood.   I must have been in shock.   *How I could have missed all that happened around me?   It was a mystery to us all.* Looking like the last man standing, I was the only person still on his feet as the bouncers and the security team rushed their way up the stairs to greet me.   They were checking me over, as the other guys secured the gun from the gunman.   They confirmed that he was dead before I took notice that Bradley lay bloody at my feet.   Behind me was Crystal still brandishing her gun that was trained on the gunman.

"Miss, he is no longer a threat.   He's dead." The head security officer said, attempting to assure us all that the threat was over.   The place was safe and suddenly calm as it was deafeningly quiet, and Bradley would be needing medical treatment immediately.   "You can lower your weapon now."

"Are you sure the bastard is dead?   He's good at faking lots of things."   Crystal said, sluggish to get to her feet. "I think you should stab a fork in him, make sure he's done."

Miranda was at my feet tending Bradley's wound, putting pressure on his shoulder where the biggest concentration of blood was forming a puddle.

Crystal was already emptying her gun of the two spent shells and reloading two new ones. Thankfully, she placed the gun back in her purse.   I thought for certain she might decide to empty the two rounds into the corpse for good measure.

All that happened so fast, never graced my memory again.   To my great surprise, my life was saved that night.   As Miranda recalled the events to me, my brother Bradley, quick on his feet and quicker to react, shielded my body with his own. He managed to detect the moment of truth just as I froze to the floor, he leapt in front of me catching the bullet in his left shoulder.   Crystal dove to the floor, with gun in hand, taking aim, she put two rounds in the gunman's chest.   Though her gun only held two rounds, the .45 caliber made big holes in the man, killing him within seconds.

"Mike."   Crystal called to me, showing more calm than any of us.   "You need to check on the girls."

"The girls?"   Through all the tumultuous happenings, they had totally slipped my mind. "Yeah, of course."   As I made my way down the stairs, Crystal was right behind me with her purse in tote, ready for anything.   We made our way to the hall where the restrooms were.   Once I was able to push the door of the ladies room open, the situation looked no different than what happened upstairs.   A bleeding man was blocking the door from fully opening.   A shinny pair of golden scissors were deeply imbedded in the back of the man's leg.   As he begged me to help him, Crystal implored him to shut the hell up or she would have no trouble doing to him what she did to his partner upstairs.   She removed the gun from her purse and steadied her aim at the side of his head as he decided to lay silent until the police arrived.

Taylor was still in a state of panic with Destiny holding her in her arms on the cold tiled floor. The two were huddled together like children. As it turned out Taylor had recognized the guy leaving the men's room at the same moment she had exited the lady's room. A devious plan was in the works, and Taylor became the only problem. The man was none other than the guy who took her to Las Vegas, Bill Ray Hall, who was also the accomplice to the gunman upstairs.

At first, nothing had made any sense to me. I couldn't understand why he would come to the club just to attack Taylor. But as it turned out, it was never his idea to attack anyone. However, Billy Ray made a promise to help an old friend. Little did he know, he was being played as the patsy. The moment Billy Ray was discovered by Taylor, the two of them panicked. While trying to keep Taylor quiet, she attempted to scream making the situation more volatile. Inundated with the fear of being caught, Billy Ray made the huge mistake of shoving Taylor back into the restroom, muffling her screams with his hand across her mouth. Just as the shots from upstairs rang out, Taylor tried to scream for help. The other ladies in the restroom flooded out of the restroom never noticing or caring about the man trying to stifle her. Unfortunately, she couldn't be heard from within the tiled walls of the restroom while every lady in the building was also, screaming for freedom and safety. About the time Taylor bit the inside of Billy Ray's hand, was when Destiny arrived detecting her friend in need, not knowing the situation or being able to see clearly, Destiny did as her instincts ruled. Groping through her purse, she found the only sharp weapon available to her at the time. Destiny, with her poor vision working against her, couldn't see why Taylor was screaming so violently. The vision she had previously, led her to believe that her friend was being raped by a stranger in the lady's room. With the scissors in hand, she thrust them deep in the back of the leg of the man who was already bleeding from his bite wound. Not until the man hit the floor would Destiny stop twisting and pushing the scissors deeper into his hamstring, just as Crystal had instructed weeks earlier at work. No doubt, Crystal was very good at offering advice on self protection.

Though the immediate danger might have been over, it was obvious that something was seriously wrong with Taylor. Even as Destiny did her best to console and comfort her, it did no good trying to calm her from the panicked state that besieged her. She could hardly recognize any of us except for Destiny. And even she had trouble calming her down from the hysterics that seemed to possess Taylor .

"We got this, you need to greet the police and make sure everyone is okay upstairs," Crystal said with a wink and a nod, keeping steady aim with her gun." Obviously, she didn't want to panic Destiny by announcing that Bradley had been shot and would need tending to.

"Good idea." I was still in a foggy state of shock. My sister's hands were drenched with the man's blood. I ran up the stairs, leaping several steps at a time. Still in place was my security crew keeping steady vigil over my family. I knelt to Bradley's side where Miranda was keeping steady pressure on his wound. I called out to one of my security team, "I need one of you to tend to the girls in the rest room." Slowly I gained back some of my senses. "Don't worry brother, the girls are fine, but the guy who tried to tangle with your girl got the sharp edge of golden scissors.   You saved my life, brother."

"Yeah, well, somebody had to stop the bullet."

"I can't believe how fast you reacted.   I don't even remember you getting up, much less you shielding me."   I was relieved to see Bradley in good spirits.   I couldn't imagine what it must have felt like having a bullet in the shoulder.   And from such close range, *it must have kicked like a mule.*

"Once I saw Crystal give me the signal, I simply reacted."

"She signaled you?"

"Just like Rambo.   With gun in one hand, she held up three fingers with the other, counting down her fingers to attack.   She put two slugs in Peter before he knew what hit him.   Ya know she shot him from between your legs?   My ears are still ringing."

"That old mug was Peter?   Peter Walbrook who is supposed to be tucked away safely in Jail? Well that makes sense why Billy Ray would be here."

Bradley suddenly became alerted to the dangers Destiny had warned him of involving the return of Billy Ray.   "Where are the girls?   Are they okay?"

"Yeah, of course.   Destiny and Crystal are with Taylor downstairs.   She'd be here at your side if Taylor hadn't met up with Billy Ray. But, don't panic. Nothing a sharp pair of scissors couldn't take care of."

Miranda smiled in jest.

"You know you could have told me something, given me a bit of a hint as to what was to come."   I said, looking at Miranda.

"And had I done that you would be the one

waiting for the coroner."   Miranda mocked,   "You know the rules as well as I do.   Timing is everything…what right would I have to interfere with that?   I think everything went rather well considering Bradley will be needing a new shirt and some attention in the ER."

"And Taylor will be needing a lot of attention from Destiny.   Did my sister ever discuss that with you, Bradley?"

"Already ahead of you, brother.   We knew this would be the day that Taylor
would gain back her memory of the rape and attack on her husband.   It was just a matter of time--"

"And similar circumstances."   I added.

"Did he try to--"   Miranda inquired with a sudden look of distain.

"I don't think so.   It was merely similar circumstances that caused her to recall the past."

As the three of us discussed the nature of Taylor's amnesia, both the ambulance and police arrived filing into the place like ants to a picnic.   It didn't take them long to find Crystal with her gun ready, willing and, this one being, able.   A long standing joke existed between Crystal and myself.   She had named all three of her guns.   Whence, Ready, Willing and Able.   I believe Able was with her on this particular day.

While the security crew gave their statements to the police, the investigators were jotting every bit of information down.   The medical personnel was helping Bradley to the gurney.   While I was able to see from my vantage point, a handcuffed guy with a very bad limp struggling his way out the door with the assistance of a, less sympathetic, cop.

At some point we all seemed to gather at the lower level on the dance floor.   Taylor was extremely emotional as Destiny would go from

Bradley then back to her.   My sister had her hands full.   They readied Bradley for travel soon after it was decided that Destiny would transport in the ambulance with him.   Miranda then turned her attention to Taylor.   Her emotional state was off the charts.   At one point, the poor girl actually thought that the police were there to take her away.   It was all that we could do to keep her from incriminating herself.   Miranda worked with her, taking her aside, hoping to keep her silent long enough to get her home.

         Soon after Bradley and Destiny were taken away, I saw Crystal acting strangely.   Something was wrong.   It wasn't like her to become ill from such an event.   She was more the warrior type than any of us.   One of the cops in the building asked if she was alright.   In the attempt to continue with the investigation, Crystal became violently ill.   Amid sentence, she clutched at her stomach and fell to her knees.   I saw the event unfold before my eyes a split second before her head hit the floor.   I rushed to her side just as she passed out with her head landing safely in my lap.   I had no idea what had happened to her, but I wasn't going to let anything come between us.   I demanded someone call for an ambulance.   I held her at the center of the dance floor tucked in my arms.   Never before had I ever seen her so far from being in control.   I thanked God that it was me who was holding her.   I could feel the emotional bond that we once shared.   I begged God to make sure nothing would happen to her.   Though there were no obvious signs of trauma, I worried how that son of a bitch, Peter might have found a way to get to her after all.   He could have done a number of things that we never would have detected.   Had he gone in the kitchen, he might have poisoned her food. The possibilities were endless.   My mind fell frantic hoping that she would survive the day unscathed.   I couldn't wake her.   She was unconscious.   What could have caused this to happen to her?   I needed Miranda's help, but she wasn't able to leave Taylor. I sat on the floor holding Crystal in my arms feeling helpless and confused.   I rocked her as I spoke to her, promising she would be okay.   Though the words were empty, I prayed they were not.   The time it took the ambulance to arrive seemed an eternity.

CHAPTER 19
The beginning of the end.   Part 5

Finally, the ambulance arrived at the club.   It was accompanied by the fire department and another paramedic.   More police arrived due to the fact that we called for additional medical help.   *Where were they when Crystal was passed out in need of emergency care?*   I knew the delay in her receiving treatment might have hampered any possibility of her surviving the attack.

Immediately, the paramedics took her vitals and checked her heart.   It took Miranda and Taylor awhile to make their way over to me.   Taylor was emotional wreckage, in no way able to fend for herself.   That was obvious.

"Is it possible that she could be pregnant?" The paramedic questioned me.

"No, of course not."   I said, thinking what a stupid question to be asking at such a time.

"Yes, she could be."   Miranda, said, contradicting me, just like a woman.

"Wait, she could be?"   *...How could that be?* Miranda smiled in response.

"We will need to transport her now.   Will anyone be riding along?"   The paramedic was being as pragmatic and efficiently quick as I could stand.

I looked to Miranda who nodded for me to go.   "That would be me."   I looked back at Miranda as the gurney was scissor lifted back to full height.   "Will you two will be okay?"

"We will be fine.   Crystal needs you, Honey.   Take care of her, and I will take care of Taylor."

Like a fast moving train, too fast to imbibe every bit of information that would come to pass, the events of the night were dizzying and stressful. While in the ambulance the paramedics assured me that Crystal was doing fine, however, the concern for the baby was equally paramount.   Somehow, they were able to confirm that Crystal was, indeed, pregnant.   She was twenty weeks along according to the hospital who dispatched the information over the radio.   I couldn't believe it, *Crystal pregnant?*   It never occurred to me.   We all knew the day would come, but not so soon.   Or perhaps this was just my chauvinistic manhood glowing to blindness as Miranda would say.   So who was the dad?   Was Bob a bigger secret than I first thought? Miranda…I thought to myself.   *That girl holds more secrets than all of the WW 2.   Nobody tells me anything.*

The ride in the ambulance took less than ten minutes, all the while, Crystal never regained consciousness.

As we arrived at the hospital, Crystal was whisked away from me.   I was made to wait in the waiting room for, what seemed to be hours, when finally, a doctor came from behind the double doors. He located me and approached with a favorable nod. "She will be fine."   was all I heard him say.   All the other information seemed incidental and most secondary to the fact that she had just been through quite a horrific ordeal for someone who was pregnant.   I thanked the doctor for taking the time to speak with me.   I was still made to wait for Crystal to be cared for before anyone could visit with her. While waiting in a fog filled-daze, a gentleman sat next to me.   I was so entranced in thought, I hadn't realized it was Bob.

"Hey, I thought you were out of town."   I said with a frog in my voice, not realizing how tired I was until I tried to speak.

"I was.   Any word yet?"   Bob showed great concern as I would have expected from a possible expectant daddy.

Hesitant to go into any detail, I answered, "Aside from her being exhausted and depleted of fluids, they said she should be fine."   My memory seemed to serve for the most part.   "They are making her stay the night for observation, and we should be able to visit any minute."   I didn't know how much to say or ask.   "How did you hear about what happened at the club?”

"Your wife.” Bob answered, nodding his head. "She's looking for a parking spot as we speak. She insisted on my coming in ahead. She's quite a pushy girl."

"Yep,” That had me smiling. "that she is."

Miranda found her way into the waiting room, sitting on the other side of me. With her Nokia car-phone still in hand she asked if there had been any changes.

"Since five minutes ago? Nothing new. Relax. Take a breath.” I said, as Miranda was slow to catch her breath. Apparently, she had run the entire distance into the waiting room. The telescoping antenna of the phone was still protruding like a jousting weapon. Calmly, I took the phone from her hands before the flimsy metal of the antenna could happen to get bent like the three others we, somehow, managed to break.

Just then, Destiny came from the emergency room with a promising look on her face. She looked to be exhausted and beat, but she kept her strength.

Intercepting any questions from the three of us, Destiny was quick to state what she knew so far. "Bradley is fine. No broken bones. He lost only a small amount of blood. Thank you, Miranda." Destiny briefly hugged my wife showing her sincere gratitude for her love and her know how. *It's always good to have a doctor in the family.* "He won't be needing any transfusions, provided the surgery goes well, and they don't see any reason why it wouldn't. He should be out of surgery in an hour, and they will let us know if he needs to stay the night.

"He could be coming home tonight?" Miranda marveled.

"If all goes well." Destiny took a deep

breath.   Her hands were still visibly shaking.   "If you guys would prefer, you don't need to stay.   I know it's been a long night for all of us.   I can call if you if anything comes up."

"Firstly,"   Miranda said, immediately protesting the mere thought of abandoning her.   "we wouldn't leave you here alone for any reason.   So you're stuck with us whether you like it or not."   Miranda paused a moment to strategize her words without sounding overwhelmingly worrisome.   "We are actually here for two reasons."

Destiny gave an odd look as she began to self-sooth herself by rubbing her hands.   If I didn't know any better I might have guessed that she was performing a psychometric evaluation of what Miranda might be saying, almost trying to read the words before they were spoken.

"They said it was nothing too serious, but they felt it would be wise for Crystal to stay the night for observation and some tests."

"Tests?   Observation?   What happened? She was fine when we left the club."   Destiny's concern was quite evident.   They had grown very close over the past few months.   It would seem Crystal had grown on all of us.   Her barrier wall was slowly diminishing with each day's passing.   It was a warm feeling to see such concern for Crystal, coming from people who were complete strangers just months before.

"She's been working herself pretty hard. Between her work at the two companies and going to school, she left little energy for herself."

"No doubt, it would take a considerable amount of energy to conduct business as she does and still leave enough time to play Rambo, going around shooting people."   I thought I would lighten the mood by adding a little levity to the situation.   "She really needs to stop playing those violent video games.   Those poor ducks."

Miranda merely rolled her eyes.

"Wow, I never thought I'd see the day the dragon lady would show any signs of weakness.   I hope she'll be okay."   Destiny said, still rubbing her hands.

"The doctors say, all she needs is some rest and she will be fine."   My thoughts were the same as Destiny's.   This truly would mark the first time, the dragon lady had collapsed due to exhaustion. She had been working herself to a frizz, and it was beginning to show it's effects on her.

"Have any of you been in to see her yet?"

"Not yet, Des.   They had to find her a room, get her dressed and all that formal stuff first."

"I've been worried about her lately.   I could see the work load catching up with her.   I hope she takes this as a sign and starts listening to us for a change. She needs to slow down."   Destiny was reading something deeper.   I could see it in her weary eyes.

"Try making her do anything that she prefers not to do, and see where that gets you."   Bob remarked, remorsefully.

"True."   The three of us said, simultaneously.

Just then, Destiny showed near signs of panic. "Where is Taylor?   Is she okay?"

"She's with DJ.   I took her home on the way here.   She's taking it all pretty hard though. Fortunately, we've all been alerted to this day." Pacifying the situation momentarily, Miranda knew there would be many days of recovery time needed for Taylor.

Bob's perplexing look gave hint to what was on his mind.   "What happened to her?   I thought no one else got hurt."

Miranda was first to reiterate the situation, explaining an ugly past in Taylor's life that had yet to unfold.   There was hardly a need or reason to speak of the event till we knew we would need to address and treat the inevitable accordingly.   Without going into too much legal detail, Miranda doled enough information to paint a pretty picture of Taylor's past.

We could see the words written all over Bob's face before he spoke a word.   It was obvious he was quite taken by her, and was saddened by the situation she now faced.

With concern written on his face, Bob offered his hand at helping the young girl.   "Not that all of you haven't already covered all the bases, I would offer the company psychologist to help with her if you think it might help with any of her emotional needs."   Bob was genuinely kind as he was insightful.   We all understood what Taylor was in dire need of, but it couldn't come from anyone but family.   This bit of cover-up would never sit well with any jury, should such facts become public.

"Yes, the bases have been covered.   And thank you for the offer.   That was very sweet of you to offer, but this is something, we as family, will need to work out.   Especially with all the personal ramifications involved."   Miranda now had a few questions brewing in the cauldron of her curious mind.   "That was very kind of you.   Just a small question, Bob."

"Oh, here it comes."   I knew it.   Miranda was just getting warmed up when she would make little of any question.

"Why do you go by the name, Bob?"
...Because that's what his mommy named him.
Miranda threw us all a curve ball with that one.
Why the sudden inquiry delving into the man's

personal life?

"It was always easier in the business world to use Bob as my name."

"And the company psychologist would be the company that both you and Crystal work at, *together*?"

Bob, looked to be wondering what she was driving at with this odd line of questioning.   "Of course."

Destiny had already put things together, but I was still dealing with a few black pages in my own interrogation report.   "I thought…*we* thought you were a traveling salesman.   Do you mean to tell me your first name is Roberto?"

"That would be true.   Robert or Roberto.   And yes, I am a salesman, even though Crystal prefers to refer to me as her very own personal escort."

We all looked to be deep in thought.

"Why are all of you looking at me like that? I feel as though I'm about to be burned at the stake or something."   Bob inquisitively looked at both of us.

"Sorry, pal.   We had no idea you were working with Crystal all this time."

"Would that make some kind of a difference?"   Bob seemed rather confused.

"No, not at all."   I tried to explain.   "It would seem our darling Crystal had been keeping secrets from us.   It's a long story, actually.   When this is all over, we need to talk with you about a few things."

"Amen to that."   Destiny agreed.   This time, without the wine glass.   Instead, she offered a high-five to Miranda.

Chapter 20
Roberto's awakening

  It all began to make perfect sense after
Roberto explained his true name and origin.
Roberto Tuccironi, born in Italy where soon after his
birth, he and his parents moved to the USA.
  Roberto's dad was a very wealthy man,
deeply involved with the olive oil business.
  Soon after moving to the states, his dad
retired a millionaire, living rather comfortably in a
community called Calabasas.   From there Roberto
was raised and went to school where he found his
penchant in sales.   He first started out selling sports
cars such as Ferrari, Porsche and Maserati.
  The dealership, where he got his fist job as a
car washing kid, was less than two miles from his
high school, El Camino Real.   Each day after school
he would come to the Calabasas dealership.   He
spent hours gawking at the fine foreign cars on
display there.   Day after day, he was seen looking in
the windows of each model.   He seemed to have a
private love affair with the beauty and soft curves of
those exotic cars.   One day one of the salesman
decided to put Roberto to work.   With a bucket of
water in one hand and a soft chamois cloth in the
other, the man offered to pay him two dollars per
washed car, every day after school.   Roberto hastily

accepted.   It would not take long before the other guys got used to seeing him working with the cars, washing, cleaning, vacuuming and occasionally he would be asked to move the cars around the lot. Though, when he was propositioned to help work with the mechanics and maintenance of the cars, Roberto, who soon started going by the name Bob, as it seemed easier for others to remember, politely refused the position, stating he would much prefer to be the one enlisted to sell the cars.   Needless to say, company policy precluded seventeen year-olds from driving the cars off the lot, therefore, a sales position was not possible.   But that soon changed.   Roberto had a plan.

He had a quick mind.   He learned a great deal of information by secretly watching every move of the other salesman on the lot.   He kept mental notes of every successful sale and what it took to convince the buyer to follow through with a purchase.

Most of the exotic cars on the lot boasted price tags nearing one-hundred thousand dollars. Roberto reasoned that if a person was remotely tempted to come to the lot and take a test drive, there was absolutely no reason why any of those people wouldn't be in the position to purchase one of those fine beauties as well.   So the one thing, in his mind, holding back a potential purchase, would only be the shortcoming of the salesman himself.   It was only too obvious to him that a good salesman could make the deal just as easily as break the deal.

He studied the psychology behind the purchase of an expensive sports car as opposed to the mundane practicality of other cars.   It didn't take him very long before he felt confident enough to make sales of his own.   He had such a passion for the cars, he believed he would be capable of transferring that same elated enthusiasm when showing the cars to potential buyers.   All he needed was the chance to get his foot in the car door…so to speak.

Like many times before, Roberto would be tending to the cars in the lot before any of the salesman had noticed a potential buyer strolling through the lot.   Though his impetuous actions could easily have gotten him fired, he took the chance most people would not dare think to do.   It was a chance he felt was well worth taking.

The young novice, grabbed a jacket he had stashed in the trunk of one of the show cars.   He confidently approached the man and presented one of his favorite cars to the gentleman, who seemed to be a possible candidate.   Though the man was still on the fence, Roberto, was determined to keep this guy interested.   He was an older man, recently retired and only thinking about buying a flashy sports car to show his worth from all his years of hard work. Immediately, Roberto baited the hook.   Though the price would be the only thing holding this man back from a sale, Roberto recognized the familiar hunger in any man's eye when gazing into a fine machine. From watching intently, he knew exactly how to encourage the ego of the tightest wallet.   And he added a few new lines of his own to guarantee the sale.   The confidence was bountiful.   To him it was like shooting fish in a barrel.   The gentleman didn't stand a chance from the moment he walked onto the lot.   He'd have been just as successful at resisting the purchase of that new car as he would have had taking all his money out of his savings, buried it in the back yard and watched it grow.   With all the lines delivered in perfect cadence and timing, the hook was set.   The man was ready for the next step. Had Roberto not had the confidence to proceed, this certainly would have been a terrible blunder on his behalf.   But he had already foreseen the success of this sale weeks before he ever met the man. Politely, Roberto excused himself to retrieve the keys for the second phase of the ruse; the test drive. Having already made a carefully thought out plan, the suave novice removed his jacket just out of sight of the buyer and placed it over his arm to resemble one of the trash bags he, so frequently, held when dumping the trash and conducting other various chores around the showroom floor.   With a simple nod, he greeted each of the salesmen that were still too busy doing paperwork to notice the gentleman out in the parking lot.   Of course, Robert had planned that out too.

He had the man sit in the comfort of the driver's seat, while he retrieved the keys just to help get him acquainted with the car he would soon be driving.   Heading straight to the back of the showroom, Robert made his rounds collecting the trash from each of the cans behind each desk. Methodically, he made his usual rounds gathering trash from place to place.   As he approached the desk that housed the keys to each of the cars, he nonchalantly swiped the one's he needed and pocketed them unnoticed by anyone.   Like a well planned out bank robbery, Roberto had it all worked out to the finest detail.   He had rehearsed the plan, many times before, in his head.   As he made his way out through the glass doors of the showroom, he tossed the trash bag to the side of the building, slipped his jacket back on and headed straight to the gentleman who looked to be a guy seated in a jet rocket with a glowing gleam in his eye and a dream of a possible future on his mind.   The fantasizing smile on the gentleman was priceless.   Not to say, that wouldn't come in handy at the time of signing the check.   Roberto sat himself in the passenger seat next to the gentleman.   In the cup holder at center console he placed the man's coffee.

"Two cream, no sugar, well stirred."   If there was a better word than suave in the dictionary, it would have been called, Roberto.   Slipping the keys into the ignition, he instructed the gentleman to start her up.   That's all it took, up to that point. The rest was up to the performance of the car. Fortunately, the car didn't disappoint.   Roberto made it a notable point to show the man how interested many of the other drivers were.   The jet black, shiny, brand new Maserati Biturbo SI 2500 with the majestic Trident logos was quite an impressive car to be sure.   The man's ego was fed generously at every turn and stop light.   With the hook deeply set, it was just a matter of reeling the man in with his checkbook in hand.   The car roared from the stop with an impressive rumble from beneath the hood.   With quickness, too much to compete with, the car sped from the stop light with an impressive g-force pressing our bodies against the seat with every acceleration.   And, fortunately, the man was none too shy to push the pedal with inquisitive anticipation.   The car did not let him or his insatiable ego down.

Needless to say, upon returning to the lot, Roberto had guaranteed himself his first car sale. However, in order to keep from being fired, he had to relinquish the commission back to the company as a matter of principal.   Though the loss of the commission was a sizable amount of money to be sure, ironically, the money never crossed his mind. The sale was all he was after, hitherto, the monetary gain was merely an afterthought.   The coming commission was, consequently, the topping on the cake of his new career.

The following year Roberto had achieved what was thought to be the impossible.   His sales had exceeded all expectations when he surpassed the record sales quota.   He was awarded with an assistant management position within his second year of employment.   He was a mere senior in high school, selling cars worth more than many homes in the area.   His passion grew stronger with every sale. And with every sale, Roberto's passion for exotic cars grew exponentially.   He later, graduated from high school after his first semester, hungry for opportunity.

Around the time he began thinking about owning his own dealership, he was approached by a distinguished gentleman who was in need of a new sports car.   *Need* was the opportune word.   The gentleman was very pragmatic and business like, demanding of respect and seemingly deserving of his demands.   He emanated the very essence of success and prosperity.   He was the very kind of man that Roberto would prefer to emulate.   The highly distinguished gentleman claimed to be in need of one of the cars from the lot to help persuade a member of his company, a rogue CEO, to keep from quitting and moving on to another company.   To Roberto, this kind of cogent bribery was only heard of in fairy tales and in Hollywood movies.   Roberto was highly impressed with the gesture of this gentleman, but he felt driven to take the sale one step further. Recognizing that this distinguished gentleman was more than a mere potential buyer, Roberto had taken the challenge beyond the call of duty.   Seasoned with a perfected eye of opportunity, he convinced this distinguished gentleman that nothing would impress the said rogue CEO more than to see the same car driven by his persuader.   The distinguished gentleman seemed to be pleased by the tactic of such an overtly delivered bribe.   One man might have thought that Roberto was facetiously joking.   But a better man would easily discern the potential of such reasoning and tactical thinking as a very useful tool.

"Tell me something, Son."   The distinguished man spoke, showing absolutely no emotion.   "I'm not a betting man.   If you get my meaning.   I make a business of reading people and culling straight through the façade of bullshit."   The man strategically held a pause in his demanding delivery.   Roberto made a point not to flinch or take his eyes from the distinguished gentleman's,   "I will meet your offer plus raise you double your commission under one condition."   Like an opponent in a high stakes poker game, the man's face could not be read.

Roberto fed eagerly on the challenge.   This was obviously an opportunity many would never see coming in a lifetime.   "And that would be?"   He said, already emulating the gentleman's demeanor.

"Your potential as a salesman is obviously not being met or challenged here."   Purposefully, the distinguished gentleman paused once more.

"Go on…"   Roberto's eagerness could only be regarded as a potential interest in the man's offer which Roberto made certain would not be misconstrued as greed or naivety.

"Collect your commission and give your notice here as of now.   Come work for me and I will see what we can do about getting you a real paycheck working with real sales."

In less than a heartbeat, Roberto's mind was already working to gain his own personal repertoire of success through the offerings of the very distinguished gentleman.

With a mere gentleman's handshake, the deal was settled and sealed.   "You have a deal."

Roberto held out his hand.   "Roberto Tuccironni."

"Mr. Worthington, to you until you can beat me at racquetball."   The two shook hands. Never once, did the man tip his hand with any facial expressions.   He simply retrieved a business card from his fob, handing it to Roberto.   He said, "Report to this young lady eight A.M. sharp tomorrow morning.   She will set you up with Armani and such.   We keep a high standard not to be challenged by tattoos, fake jewelry or cheap clothes.   I'm sure you understand."

Roberto nodded in response, instantly recognizing the business name of the company.   "I understand.   If you don't mind me asking, what exactly will I be selling to your clientele?"

Mr. Worthington was virtually answering the question before Roberto was able to get the words out.   "Does it really matter, son?"

A smile slowly grew across Roberto face.   It was as though a sudden kindred epiphany occurred. "No…I suppose not."

The two entered the showroom to finalize the paperwork of the two cars that Mr. Worthington had just purchased.   And as agreed, Roberto gave notice, sealing his fate.

Samantha once said, a good salesperson is one who will pour, add sugar and cream, stir and serve your coffee without taking his eyes from yours. A true salesperson, however, is one who already believes he had made the sale before offering you a beverage.

CHAPTER 21
Semorray

With the tables turned, and the three of us being the keepers of a secret, we all felt very elated to know and finally realize we had found Mr. Right. And what a secret he, too, would soon learn. If it hadn't been for the fact that we were at the hospital waiting to hear vital results, we might have been celebrating loud and jolly.

The nurse came to the waiting room asking for those who came with Crystal. The four of us leaped to our feet in response. Understanding hospital protocol, we looked to each other allowing the other to go ahead for the first round of visitation.

"She has her own private room." The nurse said, gesturing with a wave. "All of you can come."

"Thank you. How is she?" Miranda nearly begged to hear.

"She's fine, but you can ask her for yourself. She's right around here." The nurse quickly guided us through the labyrinth of rooms, leading us to the darkened halls of the hospital. "You have guests, my dear." The nurse announced, busily refilling the ice water and placing the bed controls within Crystal's reach.

We must have looked like clowns wondering who would speak first. "Hey, was it really so necessary to scare us like this?" Miranda said, reaching for Crystal's hand. Destiny rushed to the other side of the bed placing her hand on Crystal's shoulder.

"It wasn't quite the plan." Crystal had an unfamiliar groggy tone to her voice.

"She's been sedated." said the nurse, quickly responding to our reactions.

"How do you feel?" Destiny said, offering a

smile that was hiding something monumental.

"Aside from the obvious, I feel rather well. It's not every day one gets to empty her gun in public."

"Wow, that was unexpected."   Destiny spouted.

"Spoken like a true mercenary."   Roberto added, coming out from the shadows to greet his girl.

The look on Crystal's face said it all.   *Like Daddy was home for Christmas,* she smiled with her eyes as her lips were slow to follow suit resulting from the sedation.

"If you need anything, Hon, just press the button."   The nurse announced as she headed for the door.

"Could you let me know when Bradley Wiki gets out of surgery?"   Destiny said.

"Sure, love.   What room was he assigned?"

"I'm not sure.   He came in by ambulance and went straight to surgery.   Gun shot wound."

"I can find out for you."   In a flash, the nurse disappeared from sight.

Miranda moved aside allowing Roberto to come closer.

"I'm surprised to see you back so soon." Crystal said.

"Nothing a company jet and a two hour cab ride couldn't remedy."   He held her hand in both of his.   "I could go back to work if you prefer."

"To hell with that shit, fella.   I'm not you letting go."   Sounding like a drunk dyslexic, Crystal tried to keep her composure.

"Wow, I like this Crystal."   Destiny marveled, never having heard this side of her before. "Dragon lady has a heart underneath all that brass after all."

"Crystal put her and Roberto's fingers to her

lips.   "Shhh, what happens in this bed stays in this bed…I think that's what I meant."   Crystal was hardly able to keep from slurring.   *No doubt, they must have had a hard time keeping her from trying to escape once she came to.   Sedation must have been the only resolve.*

"I want double of whatever they gave you, sister."   Destiny announced.

I cast a brotherly protective sneer at my sister.

"Don't make ugly."   Destiny backhanded my shoulder.   "It's not for me.   I would use it to slip in her tonic and lime the next time she slams my poor Bradley."

"Bradley is a Dork."   Crystal proudly rebutted as she burped aloud.

Miranda covered her mouth holding back her vicarious embarrassment.

As perfectly timed as anyone of her drunk acts, Crystal was entertaining to say the least.   It was a side of her few of us had ever witnessed.

"You look like hell.   Didn't they feed you on that nasty jet?"

"Y Tu sei la donna piu bella che io abba mai visto.   (And you are the most beautiful woman I've ever seen.)   Who could think of food with you here in the hospital?"

"We're in America.   Speak American."

"You could have told me sooner."

"And spoil the farty…party?"

The esoteric implications became less confusing as they continued.

"Something could have gone wrong.   And I would not have been there to protect you, Bella."

"I don't need protecting,"   barked Crystal, tussling with the sheets that seemed to be smothering her midsection.   "Besides, the timing would not have worked as planned with you there."

Destiny tried to keep her cool as a festering curiosity seemed to pervade.   "You already knew? And said nothing to any of us?"

"Too much was at stake for her to divulge anything."   I said, while attempting to put more pieces together as well.

"And you knew, too?"

"Not right away."

"Wow, I thought *I* had the gift."

"You do."   Miranda said.   "We saw that big grin on your face not five minutes   ago."   Miranda turned to Crystal.   "So when were you planning on letting the rest of us in on your little secret?"

"Secret?"   Crystal said, playing out her habitual obstinacies.

"You know…"   Miranda looked to Destiny for confirmation.   "Doesn't she?"

Destiny nodded with a   positive smirk in response.

"You brat.   Why would you keep this a secret from us?"

"Timing is everything…bla, bla, bla.   You guys know the drill.   Why would you even bother to ask?"

"Wow, so many secrets.   Do any of us know the full story?"

"Stop with the *'wow'* already."   Crystal barked at Destiny.   "You sound like my kindergarten teacher.   "Say, holy shit or, what the fuck.   Nobody except for Bradley says wow or groovy or some geeky shit like that."

"I think she needs another round in her IV."   Destiny retorted, defending her man.

"Okay, we got this far without causing any paradoxical disasters."   Miranda announced, demanding Crystal's undivided attention.   "Can we make it official now?”

“Shit, yes, you can make it official.   And I am not a brat.”   Crystal grabbed the IV hose to shake it at us.   “I think we’re gonna need more octane in this juicer thingy.   I can still see nagging people.”

“If not a brat, I suppose I could think of a few better names should you prefer.”   Destiny said, showing more of her combative side.

“I bet you could.”   Crystal said, with the patented smirk peeking through the corner of her mouth.

“Does everyone in the room know the truth?” Miranda asked, wondering if Roberto had already known as well.

“If you are implying the tall Italian named Roberto Tuccironi, the answer is yes, fuck yes.” Roberto was only too proud to share his smile with us all.

“You are incorrigible.”   Miranda barked. “Both of you.”

“And, I’m twenty weeks along.   Did you really think I wouldn’t be getting pre-natal care by now?   Shit, people, it was hard enough hiding the baby bump from all of you, much less keeping Destiny’s groping fingers off of me.   And let me tell you, Donna Karan does not do well with bumps. My entire wardrobe is a disaster.”

“Can I, at least, grope now?”   Destiny said, looking like she would towards a massive bowl of chocolate bars on Halloween.

“Grope away…”   Crystal threw back the sheet revealing a tiny baby bump beneath her gown.

“Oh, look how cute.”   Destiny started in with the cooing.   Come here, cute little baby bump.”

“Really, is it going to be like that?”   Crystal grimaced, already criticizing the nauseating baby talk.

"Better get used to it, Momma."   Destiny said, placing her hand on the little bump that had previously been so well hidden from us all.

Her glowing smile was all the evidence we needed.   Even bigger than before, her smile warmed all our hearts at once.   The emotions ran amok, with tears streaming down both her cheeks.   The vibration revealed all the secrets.   Destiny saw it all like words on the pages of a novel, spewing to overflow with happiness, joy, and of course, the memory of everything Rosemary was to each of us. She then called Roberto to her side.   Less hesitant than he might have been before, Roberto stood at Destiny's side without a clue as to what would come of it.   With her hand still placed on Crystal's tummy, she reached with her other hand for his wrist. As she firmed her grip we could see the transformation in his eyes.   It was though he were holding his little girl for the very first time.   Lost in a dreamlike state, Roberto smiled proudly.   For all we knew he might have been witnessing his daughter winning her first spelling bee, or riding her bike without the aid of training wheels.   Whatever the case, we all saw it in his smiling eyes.   There was no denying it.   The pride and glory was written all over his face as well.   Witnessing such a joyous miracle brought tears to my wife's eyes.

Like a young child unwilling to wait her turn to receive presents from beneath the Christmas tree, Miranda came to the other side of the bed as well. With just her hand placed on Destiny's shoulder, she too read deeply into the visions that flooded their emotions from brimming to overfilling.

"Can you feel this, Crystal?"   Miranda asked through the tears.

Calmly and without hesitation she said,

"Every minute of every day.   While eating my breakfast, shopping for clothes with friends, and even while brushing my teeth, Rose is with me just as she is with you at this very moment."

What might have been held back hitherto, became spontaneously unleashed like the Mulholland dam of California as the girls cried together enthralled by the vibration and the omnipresence of Rosemary and her eternal love for all of us.   The sensory of perception that they so freely received was filled with laughter, joy, the sorrows of the past and the happiness of the future.   Like entering a gateway to heaven, they all were able to visit where angels lived and loved everyday.

"Have you thought of a name for her yet?" Miranda said, wiping away the tears.

"Semorray."   Proudly, Crystal answered.

"That's really pretty.   That sounds kind of familiar.   Does the name have special meaning?"

Destiny didn't need Bradley's help with this riddle.   "It's Rosemary with the letters rearranged."

"Oh, you got me crying all over again." Miranda said, reaching into her purse for a tissue.

"Did I come at a bad time?"   The obnoxiously inopportune voice came from the doorway.

"Just in time, these weirdo's are molesting me."   Crystal said, showing a bit more slur to her words.   "Help, help."

The officer entered the room waiting for a sober answer from somebody.   "I could come back later."   Said the officer, looking at his watch suggesting only a few minutes would suffice.

Immediately, Bob became protective and very much in control.   "What's this about officer?"

The mere question served as a positive

answer to the officer who took the opportunity to slip on a pair of rubber gloves.   "A formality that went overlooked at the Shot of Gold."   the cop said, walking towards Crystal.

In an instant, Roberto was already between the cop and his girl,   "Is there something I can help you with?   Certainly, whatever *you* may have forgotten could be dealt with at a later, more appropriate time."

"It's okay, Honey.   It's just the help bringing me my douche bag and drain cleaner."   The drunken words coming from Crystal eerily reminded me of the many stories Destiny would tell me about Rosemary while working as a janitor.

"I can see that *she* has been tipping the bottle this evening."   The snide remark from the overbearing cop affected all of us with unfavorable spite and anger.

"She's been sedated, Officer Randall."   Roberto was less than kind with quoting the cop's name.   "And she has also gone through a harrowing experience this evening."   Roberto stood between the cop and his every attempt to look beneath the bed.

"I'm not officer as drunk you think am I."   Crystal was pouring on the Rosemary repertoire.

"Of course, you're not, Honey."   The cop was as rude as he was hasty to find something."

"Obviously, you were not in attendance at the Shot of Gold this evening when Crystal gave her statement and then was taken by ambulance to this hospital.   She is the victim of this heinous crime if in case the detective in charge forgot to inform you, *Officer Randall.*"

"That would be the very reason I am here."   The cop could see he wasn't going to get any closer to the bed without having to physically move the man who opposed him.   "And your name is?"

"I am Roberto Tuccirino.   You minchia fredda.   (spineless pussy)"   Spoken as though the cop should have already known him.

"Well, Mr. Tuccironi, I will be out of your hair as soon as I can retrieve the weapon Crystal used to defend herself."

We all looked to one another with no idea. Then we looked at Crystal who was harboring a very mischievous grin.   "Able is resting comfortably in my purse where she belongs…right next to my switch blade and my wet panties."

Each of us looked beneath the bed, simultaneously saying,   "The gun is here in the hospital?"

I had a sudden thought that struck fear up my spine that had me worried.   *Would it be possible that the damn cop might arrest Crystal for having a concealed weapon on her?*

The cop reached with his gloved hand for the purse that sat on the floor in a plastic pull-string top hospital bag.   Placing the bag on the corner of the bed, he untied it and dumped the contents out.   As sure as day, the Louis Vuitton purse stood out among her clothes that were spackled with Bradley's blood.

"Room service really sucks here."   Crystal looked to Roberto with a whisper in her voice, "Could you tell the help to come back later when we're not about to have nasty sex?"   Any other time the drunk routine would have been hilarious.

Ignoring Crystal's babbling, the cop continued with his search.   Thinking twice about dumping the purse onto the bed, he reached in. From within the depth of the designer bag he revealed a custom chrome plated double barreled, pearl handled Derringer.   With the push of a button, he breached the barrel exposing two unused shells. He tipped the gun dropping the shells to the mattress.

"We wouldn't want any accidents here in the hospital." he said, placing the gun into a plastic bag of his own.

"Make sure the butler knows to have Able cleaned and oiled before he returns her."   Crystal burped once more, seemingly annoyed that a damn burp would dare to interrupt her.   "Daddy paid good money for her, always insisting I take good care of her."

"Ballistics will need to run some tests to finalize the report."

"You just make sure to keep her shafe."   Crystal slurred.   "Paul McCartney told me that happiness is a warm gun."   She pointed a wavering finger at the cop.   "Bring her home shafe…safe and warm.   Spineless pushy…that's funny."   she said, seeming tickled with herself.

Roberto's face suddenly fell flushed listening to her babble.   Though he said nothing, the look on his face was curious enough.

The detective will call you when he has completed his report."   The cop handed Roberto a business card.   "Don't leave town…any of you." With that, he left the room.

"Aren't you going to say goodbye?"   Crystal hollered.   "Spineless pushy."
No sooner had he gone, I took a deep breath.   "What an asshole."   I abruptly spoke aloud.

"Spineless pussy…"   Crystal slurred one last time with big eyes and a waver to her head.   We had all seen that same playful silly look on Rosemary's face many times before.

"You've been playing me all along." Roberto looked to be stern with her.

"Daddy didn't raise no fool."   She said, looking a bit less inebriated.   "Facciamo una bella scopata!   (Let's have a nice fuck!)"

"Sto per fare I gattini.   (I think I'm gonna be sick.)   Roberto said, running his fingers through his thick head of jet black hair.   "All along?   The entire time?"

"High school.   Foreign language.   You're not gonna be mad are you?"

Roberto didn't look to be the least bit mad, but apparently he had been thinking that he had the market on his home language.   "Totto a posto. (everything's cool).

"Benissimo.   (Great).   Vuoi scopare?   (Do you want to fuck?)"

"You are quite the faker."   Almost but not quite taken by her guile and slyness, Roberto offered a half smile.

"And not the least bit drunk or sedated either."   I just had to call her on her game. "Douche bag, drain cleaner?   That shit was really funny.   I should be taking notes, Crystal."

"Yeah, and all of you enjoyed it…admit it." Crystal dropped the slur and the act in a nanosecond.

Destiny's mouth was agape since the cop first entered the room.   "You talked that way to a cop on purpose?"

"I know.   Wasn't that fun?   Should we call him back?"

"You really are incorrigible."   Miranda remarked, only now able to laugh at what had just transpired.

"Not me…the little devil inside me." Crystal used her innocent little Georgia girl accent.

"Oh, really?   Is it going to be like that?" Destiny teased.

"That's an eerie thought."   I remarked aloud, again.

"What's that?"   Miranda looked to hear my incidental thought.

"Little devil…Rosemary's baby?"

"Now you're starting to sound like the Brainman."   Crystal laughed, placing her hand gently on her tummy.   "My little devil.   And with all my heart.   We're all devils at heart really.   So what's my answer, big man?   Ho voglia di montare. (I'm in the mood to screw.)"

We could only imagine what she was saying to Roberto.   But I instantly recognized that familiar tone in her voice.

CHAPTER 22
Bradley's awakening

"I have a guest you might be interested in." The nurse said, returning to the room.   Following behind was Bradley sporting a new sling with his left arm wrapped in it.

"Wow…I mean groovy.   I thought you would be in recovery."   Destiny purposely used the opportunity to harass Crystal.   She gently hugged him and gave him a soft kiss on the lips.

"He never underwent anesthesia.   The wound didn't warrant it."   The nurse said, placing her hand on his shoulder as she pivoted around him before leaving the room.

"Why is it everyone seems to feel the need to pet you?"   Grimacing, Crystal fell back into her spiteful routine.   "Were you a homeless dog in a past life?"

"Ya know?   I saw a cop in the hall back there.   I was so tempted to tell him that you were the one who shot me."

“So what stopped you, Dork?”

Bradley shook his head with no retort,   “I don’t know.”

Roberto was the next to practically leap toward Bradley, offering a hand shake and a one-armed hug.   “Give the man a break, Crystal.   He’s been through enough tonight.   And from what I hear, quite the hero.   I am forever in your debt.”

“No, it was nothing.”   Bradley said, showing a real change in him.

“Not a time to be modest, brother.   Your quick reflexes saved all our butts.”   It was true, what I said.   It had to have been with lightening reflexes to have caught that bullet as he did.   And thankfully didn’t harm himself more seriously.

“It was just a reflex really.   I didn’t know what I had done until after it had already happened.”   Bradley was very humble to a fault.   “I was really just following Crystal’s lead.   If anyone should be given accolades it should be her.   It happened pretty fast, actually.   But I remember seeing him going down like sack of potatoes.   Two perfect shots to the heart.   The guy didn’t stand a chance against her steady aim.   The debt is to her really.”

“Reflex or whatever.   You are the man.   We are all in your debt.   You took a bullet for me so Crystal could take her shot.”   I was next in line to hug my brother.   The room fell silent.   No doubt, we all took the moment to reflect.

Bradley hugged each of us before slowly approaching the bed.   He must have felt something in the club that night to have moved so quickly.   Or perhaps it was true what Rosemary had once told me. His quick reflexes are those   that inevitably get him into trouble, too quick for his own good sometimes. Perhaps, this was an instilled trait of past life reflexes honed and branded into his soul.   I would not have been surprised if he hadn't done the very same thing for me in all those past lives of war and battle together.   Truly, he was my hero.   And I swore never to forget his bravery.

"How are you?"   Bradley had made his way to the bed.   Without apprehension or any hesitation, he placed Crystal's hand in his.   Patiently, he waited for her answer.

"I'm pregnant.   How are you?"   Crystal seemed a bit at odds with his humbled demeanor.

"Better, now that I understand what all this has been about."   Bradley held a note of mystery with his words."

"What's what about?"

"You know…"   With a single nod, Bradley suggested she admit her ways.

"You tell me."   Crystal refused to let down her guard.

"All along it's been your posturing and guidance that got us through to this moment. This entire evening played out exactly to plan.   You showed Destiny what to do when the time would come.   And you have been strategically, infiltrating our every move since the very first day.   It's so obvious now.   I don't know how I could have missed it.   It wasn't us who needed to watch over you.   It wasn't up to us.   It was never in our power to protect you as Rosemary had asked of us.   It's been *you* all along.   *You*, who has been watching over us.   All of us.   Guiding us from the danger. Hints from you here and there…I didn't even put it all together until they were stitching me up downstairs.   The beard and the mustache made it clear that Mr. Scott never knew where Peter was all this time.   He was a nomad, a faceless stranger completely off the grid.   He understood what he was up against.   Going underground was the only way that guy could hide from you girls and the authorities. He hid himself in plain sight the entire time.   And the one time Mr. Scott would fail to find his query was when Peter disappeared off the face of the planet the moment after he escaped from jail.   You were very clever to hide all of that from us.   You and Rosemary, that is.   This was a very long standing plan of yours.   I can't begin to understand how all this psychic stuff works.   But it's not the gift of magic and mystery that you possess in your heart, Crystal.   You proved that to me beyond any doubt. You have a far greater gift to offer than anyone I have ever met.   You hide behind a mystery cloak attempting to disguise it, but I found you out. You're caught.   Face it.   Your heart is made of love.   Your gift is love.   And your goals have been met now.   It's time to let go."

Crystal looked to be mentally melting as Bradley delivered his long overdue speech.   He had obviously been giving it a lot of thought.

"I don't know how we will ever be able to thank you enough for all that you have been doing for each of us.   Just know and try to remember that we all love you.   And now it is our turn to return all the favors to you.   You have a very special gift inside of you.   I didn't get the chance to truly get to know Rosemary very well, but I plan to now.   So you better begin to understand that you need to start taking things slower.   It's no longer a life or death plan to keep vigil.   That life is over.   It's done. Now, it's all about taking good care of yourself and your new family."   Bradley raised her hand to his lips and gently kissed her.   "I just wanted to thank you for everything…for Destiny, for this family, and being there for us all, at the right time.   Because we all know…timing is everything, yada, yada, yada."

Destiny took hold of her man, kissing him

feverishly on the lips before allowing him to speak another word.   "That was amazing, baby.   You are so passionate.   Grrr…"

Crystal remained silent in the bed still taking it all in for several seconds before she retorted with something, at first, seemingly, completely off the wall.   "There was this homeless guy who, amid his itinerant search for food, going from one trash can to another, found a dollar on the ground.   He thought that perhaps he could buy some food with it.   But instead, he bought a lottery ticket.   To his surprise, that night, while looking through a liquor store window, he discovered he had won the lottery.   It was the biggest amount of the year.   Millions would be his.   Months later he was seen driving in a car. It was old, dilapidated, and dingy just as his clothes still were.   He drove that car from trash bin to trash bin searching for his dinner.   His biggest luxury was the personalized plate on the back of the car that read, PO NO MO."

"He had everything he ever needed all along." Bradley recited the ending of the story he had once heard before.

Miranda had found her way to me, cuddling and hugging.

Destiny was doing the same with Bradley as Roberto stood by Crystal's bedside rubbing and caressing her hand before giving her a gentle kiss on her lips.   The first we had ever seen between the two.

"I love you, Bella."

"Even though we are a crazy family?"

"Especially with the crazy family that apparently love you very much."

"I love them too."   Crystal paused for a moment.   "I love you, Roberto."

After planting another kiss on her lips,

Roberto decided to reminisce a favorite time of his. "I was asked recently by my silver-haired mother, when I first realized I had fallen in love with you. Do you want to know what I said?"

Crystal's eyes lit up with anticipation. "Tell me before I piss myself."

"I answered, quite matter of fact, 'she had me at gunpoint, or fuck you. I can't remember which one she drew first.'"

At that moment I couldn't remember if I had ever heard Crystal laugh out loud before. It was so beautiful to hear her laughter.

"Do you suppose that before he won the lottery the personalized plate could have read. ME SO PO?" Bradley added his personality to the mix with the moment.

"No, dork. Before winning the lottery he didn't own a car."

"Ah, there she is." Bradley laughed.

After we all had a good sobering laugh, we could see that it was the coming of sunup. The orange ball in the sky was just barely peaking over the top of the mountains.

"Did you know that Crystal spoke Italian?" Destiny asked Bradley, so impressed.

"I don't doubt it." Bradley quipped with the timing of a seasoned comedian. "She speaks more languages than that; there's her fluency in bitchiness, and her ability to chant in crablish. Let's not forget truculench, boligeon, and sarcasmanian. And of course, from her travels in the orient, she's quite versed in buttkickatwan."

"I love you too, Bradley" Crystal's banter towards Bradley would remain the highlight of our days.

Chapter 23

The following are outtakes, omissions and bloopers.   I hope you enjoy.

A Joke from Samantha;
What breed of cat often gets laryngitis?   Give up?
A meow mute!

During the time Crystal was first secretly dating Roberto Tuccironi;
Crystal and the family were at the Shot of Gold.   It was at one of the many Family Circle meetings where the family met each week.   Roberto and Bradley were heavily involved discussing quantum mechanics.   Apparently, Crystal was fed up with, and tired of the boring discussion.   "Can we talk about something more interesting?   Quantum mechanics is a set of principles underlying the most fundamental known description of all physical systems at the submicroscopic scale, particularly the atomic level.   Bla, Bla Bla."   She said, rolling her eyes.   "What more is there to say about stupid quantum mechanics?"   Just after delivering her show of resentment toward the present topic, the band had played their last note of the song.   The club was eerily quiet just long enough for all of us, seated at the VIP lounge, to hear Crystal pass gas. With every attempt to smother and hide it's

bellowing rumble, all she accomplished was to
change the tune with every wriggle of her bottom.

"And there you have it, folks, coming from a
nut shell."   Bradley, nonchalantly continued.   "A
perfect example of quantum mechanics at its finest.
I don't suppose you could get much smaller than
that."

If in case you were wondering what was in
the envelope that was from Rosemary to Bradley
with very explicit instructions for him to wait to
open;
Inside the envelope was another bandage for
the klutz, and a short congratulatory note for having
passed the bar dated the very day he got the results
from the test.

A letter came in the mail for Destiny;
The letter was from Rosemary.   It apparently had
been sent just days before from a local law office.
The letter was brail embossed.   It read,
Dearest Destiny, my sweet loving little girl, my
daughter who would never been for the timing of
mine,
We met long ago, but only for a very brief moment.
I have figured, by now you must know what I am
writing to you about.   I want, first, to congratulate
you with your success with the company.   I knew
from the times that we spoke together, you hadn't
quite figured out why I would pick you to work with
the investigative department of the insurance
company.   For obvious reasons, I could not tell you
at that time.   Secondly, I just thought I might add a
little mystery to your day; guess who your child will
be?
Love and kisses,
Rose

Miranda describes what kind of a mechanic I am to Destiny;

"Mike is quite a mechanic.   Each time the *Check Engine* light comes on, he does the right thing by immediately pulling off the road, opens the hood and checks the engine just as the manual says.   Once he locates the engine, he says, 'Yep it's still there.' And he gets back in the car and drives away going about his business."

Me at the breakfast table with Miranda and Samantha;

I was proudly searching through the local newspaper.   The review of my book had been posted.   We waited for days to read what might have been noted by the critics of my peers.   Excitedly, I read aloud to my family.   After reading about misspelled words and the ludicrous blasphemous work, my wounded heart sank, and a rather large lump in my throat crept into my protected shield of vanity and pride.   I stood up from the table in a daze.   As I walked towards the back of the house, little Samantha asked where I was going.   I somberly told her that I had a date with a tub full of water and a toaster.   Thankfully, my loving family fixed that problem.

A Joke from Crystal:
Why don't drunks make good comedians? Give up?   Because they can't do stand up.

Crystal acting out on Bradley;
Bradley had shown an interest in learning to fish.   Crystal says.   "And once you learn and become proficient, does that make you a Master Baiter?   Oh, that's right, been there done that…"

Take a guess where the term Wikipedia comes from?   Wiki-pedia.   Bradley Wiki.

Bradley also ghost writes under the name Penelope Ashe, usually accompanied with K S Michaels in the erotica genre.

Crystal acting out on Bradley;
After a brief argument with Bradley, Crystal remarks,   "If I remember correctly I was partly responsible for rescuing you from an elevator…a premature evacuation if you ask me."

Crystal acting out on Bradley;
While Crystal was in her hospital bed, she asked a favor of Bradley,   "Could you get my purse for me, please?"
"Sure, where is it?"
"Under the bed, just below me."   Crystal smirked, feeling rather proud of herself.   Roberto had already placed the purse in the closet.   We all thought curiously as to why she requested such a thing.
"I can't seem to find it."   Bradley insisted.
"Just blow me, Bradley"   Crystal laughed as she reiterated.   "Oh, that's right…the cop took my gun.   I guess you get to live."

Lucy The Third was a cute little fuzzy hamster belonging to Samantha that was kept in her room, on her dresser;
We (Our little family) liked to make it a point to tell people, that don't already know, that we don't like to talk about what happened to Lucy The Second.   Every time the subject had been brought up, the three of us folded our hands in front of us and

bowed our heads for a brief second.   "God bless her soul." Sam would whisper, shaking her head sharing a despairing mournful look.   "Let's just say we use sweepers now as opposed to vacuums."

As Bradley was being loaded onto the gurney for quick transport to the hospital, Crystal found it her public duty to remark accordingly;
Looking seriously distressed and just short of panic, Crystal rushed to Bradley's side just moments before being trundled out of the building. Looking at the paramedic in charge, Crystal says, "Please, be especially careful with this one. Though we all realize he is suffering form a traumatic flesh wound, he would, however, like us to convey his message to you that he would like to be transported with the utmost of care and consideration inasmuch as he was hoping to have sex before he dies or his fortieth birthday, which ever comes first."

A note from Samantha;
Age 15

Many have asked me for my interpretation of their dreams involving a loved one who has passed on.
Every situation is completely different from others. There could not be a single answer for all to hear or abide.   But the common scenario to come to my attention has been those who can't seem to accept the loss of a loved one and therefore seem to dream of or see the spirit of the lost love in the waking of their days.   They want resolution, finality, and answers to allow for peace to prevail.   My answer in this case to those who can't or won't let go, I say learn to let go.   Until you do, I believe your loved one may not be at peace.   I believe they just might need your

blessing to move on.   I believe love bonds an
inseparable connection that binds through eternity.
That does not mean, or give you the right to hang on
to what is not yours.   We know who we are.   If last
words never met the ears of your dearest, that's okay.
It's never too late.   If you need resolve, now is the
time.
If you have guilt, abolish it.
This is how I would do it;   make a plan.   Put aside
an evening for the spiritual healing.
May it be an anniversary or any given day of the
week, it matters not.   What is important is the act of
your resolve.   I don't believe there exists a calendar
in what might be inaccurately described as purgatory.
So pick any evening that works for you.   Know that
you are about to venture a serious healing.   While
alone or with other's who are involved, procure an
uninterrupted venue.   I would not go as far as to call
your next step a séance, but it might seem similar.
Once you have picked the appropriate date for your
healing and lit your candles, maybe sipped a bit of
wine to calm the nerves, I would simply ask that you
set aside notions of embarrassment or ego.   Make
yourself comfortable and surround yourself with a
white light.   Imagine you are a beacon waiting only
for the soul you quest.   Via your white light, you are
protected from harm and interference.   You are in a
good, safe place.   I would speak aloud asking your
spirit person of inquiry to hear you.   You needn't
wait for any replies.   This is not Hollywood or the
gypsy down the street.   Speaking aloud is not for the
benefit of your query so much, but for your sake.
Call this person aloud, tell them you need to
communicate here and now.   Tell them what is
bothering you or what you feel they need to hear (or
what you need to hear yourself say).   Make yourself
clear and understood.   If need be, write down your

thoughts beforehand and read your notes aloud if that
works better for you.   One night should be
sufficient, more than three would be counter-
productive.   You want this person to move on.
You wish them peace and love and all that applies.
Just like a coin in the wishing well, or a prayer to
God, you have cleansed the air and made your peace
with yourself and yours.   That is what I would do.

And there are times a cigar is just a cigar.

Enjoy your day.
God bless.

First print publication 2014.

Special thanks to Janette, my wonderful wife, for going far above and beyond the call of duty. You make it all worth while.   I love you very much.

Volumes of gratitude to the Ronald McDonald house of Loma Linda, California. Please, give generously to such a wonderful cause.

THANK YOU FOR SAVING MY SON'S LIFE, Loma Linda Children's Hospital of Loma Linda, California.

Thank you with all my heart, literally, to Loma Linda International Heart Institute.

First phase editing by J. Myers.   Final editing by Carol Dunn.

Special acknowledgement to Robert Dunn author of: Invasion of Long Beach, Long Beach Nights, Flawed From Inception, A Killing in The Market, Sowing in The Morning, Whispers of a Secret God, Houser Pride of America, and Proverbs of Solomon.

K S Michaels has also authored;
Love Returns Through the Portal of Time,
Love's Eclipse of The Heart
Love That Transcends Time
Erotica, Fantasy By Numbers Volume 1
When to Give Up On Life And Child
Philosophy The Obsession
My Near Death Experience
Erotica, Fantasy By Numbers Volume 2

Then Came The lightning
Out Of Justice
Out Of Revenge
Out Of Range
Out Of The Blue

To protect the privacy of those involved, this trilogy is a novel based on factual events as *The Shot of Gold* may have been shut down, it still lives on in us all, however, the names of the characters have changed. Any resemblance is purely coincidental.

K S Michaels is a steadfast survivor of over twenty-seven heart surgeries due to a congenital heart disease.   He's also a doting husband and a proud daddy.   When not writing novels, he spends much of his donated time as a motivational speaker helping parents of behaviorally challenged adolescent children, and victims of the chronically ill.   He offers accolades to Loma Linda International Heart Institute for saving his life on more than one occasion.   He grew up in Woodland Hills California, and presently resides in the High Desert of California.

The author can be reached at: ksmichaels@yahoo.com or P O Box 294846, Phelan California, 92329